Leo Tolstoy

COUNT LEO TOLSTOY was born on September 9, 1828, in Yasnaya Polyana, Russia. Orphaned at nine, he was brought up by an elderly aunt and educated by French tutors until he matriculated at Kazan University in 1844. In 1847, he gave up his studies and, after several aimless years, volunteered for military duty in the Army, serving as a junior officer in the Crimean War before retiring in 1857. In 1862, Tolstoy married Sophie Behrs, a marriage that was to become, for him, bitterly unhappy. His diary, started in 1847, was used for self-study and self-criticism, and it served as the source from which he drew much of the material that appeared not only in his great novels *War and Peace* (1869) and *Anna Karenina* (1877), but also in his shorter works. Seeking religious justification for his life, Tolstoy evolved a new Christianity based upon his own interpretation of the Gospels. Yasnaya Polyana became a Mecca for his many converts. At the age of eighty-two, while away from home, the writer's health broke down in Astapovo, Riazan, and he died there on November 20, 1910.

LEO TOLSTOY

FABLES ~ AND ~ FAIRY TALES

A NEW TRANSLATION BY
ANN DUNNIGAN

ILLUSTRATED BY
SHEILA GREENWALD

WITH A FOREWORD BY
RAYMOND ROSENTHAL

A SIGNET CLASSIC
PUBLISHED BY THE NEW AMERICAN LIBRARY

For my son, John

A. D.

June, 1962

CONTENTS

CONTENTS

FOREWORD

Leo Tolstoy wrote fables and fairy tales throughout his adult life. It is incorrect therefore to associate them solely with the later period of his writing career, when his religious conversion led him to regard what he called the "religious" and "universal" arts as the only arts worth the trouble of creation. The stories gathered in this book bear dates that stretch from Tolstoy's early manhood, soon after he had finished *War and Peace* and just before he began *Anna Karenina,* right down to the last years of his long and arduous life. True, many diverse impulses and necessities went into the making of these fables. Yet the form itself was for him a cherished one—cherished for its purity, simplicity, and directness, the qualities in both men and art he valued most—and he always returned to it, as one returns to a restful, green, beloved spot.

Like most perduring aesthetic predilections, Tolstoy's love of the fable can be traced back to his childhood. It was Nicholas, Tolstoy's eldest brother, who instilled it in him. Tolstoy has told the story of this childhood revelation so movingly that it must be quoted at length. "He [Nicholas] was a wonderful boy, and later a wonderful man. Turgenev used to say of him, very truly, that he lacked only certain faults to be a great writer. He lacked the chief fault needed for authorship—vanity—and was not at all interested in what people thought of him. The qualities of a writer that he possessed were, first of all, a fine artistic sense, an extremely developed sense of proportion, a good-natured, gay sense of humor, an extraordinary, inexhaustible imagination, and a truthful and highly moral view of life; and all this without the slightest conceit. His imagination was such that for hours together he could tell fairy tales or ghost stories or amusing tales in the style of Mrs. Radcliffe, without a pause and with such vivid realization of what he was narrating that one forgot that it was all invention. . . . It was he who, when I was five and my brothers Dmitry six and Sergey seven, announced to us that he possessed a secret by means of which, when disclosed, all men would become happy: there would be no more disease, no trouble, no one would be angry with anybody, all would love one another and all would become 'Ant-Brothers.'. . . We even organized a game of Ant-Brothers, which consisted in sitting under chairs, sheltering ourselves with boxes, screening ourselves with handkerchiefs, and cuddling against one another while thus crouching in the dark. . . . The Ant-Brotherhood was revealed to us but not its chief secret—the way for all men to cease suffering any misfortune, to leave off quarreling and being angry, and become continuously happy— this secret he said he had written on a green stick buried by the road at the edge of a certain ravine . . . there was also a certain Fanfaronov Hill, up which he said he could lead us if only we would fulfill all the appointed conditions. These were: first, to stand in a corner and *not* think of a white bear. I remember how I used to get into a corner and try (but could not possibly manage) not to think of a white bear. . . ." *

It is clear that in describing the game his brother Nicholas invented, Tolstoy has also described that magical entertainment, the fairy tale. The analogy is complete. The fairy tale's rules are like those of a game arbitrary and capricious—without imagination you can't possibly play! —but, once accepted, absolutely binding; its obstacles are delightfully mysterious and excruciating—oh, that bulky, inescapable white bear!—but, in recompense, its final rewards are vast and splendidly miraculous. To continue playing this game is, unfortunately for mankind, past the powers of most adults, yet Tolstoy did play it and perhaps more than anything else this is the proof of his genius. When he was over seventy he remembered the "green stick" in these words: "The ideal of Ant-Brothers lovingly

* Aylmer Maude, *The Life of Tolstoy*. New York: Dodd, Mead & Co., 1910, pp. 18–19.

clinging to one another, though not under two armchairs, but of all mankind under the wide dome of heaven, has remained unaltered in me. As I then believed that there existed a little green stick whereon was written the message which would destroy all evil in men and give them universal welfare, so I now believe that such truth exists and will be revealed to men and will give them all it promises." Indeed, Tolstoy felt so strongly about this that he asked to be buried at the spot where the green stick was supposed to be hidden; and after his death his wish was carried out by his wife and children.

Now Tolstoy's life is usually divided into three distinct periods: his youth, when he wrote the stories of his literary apprenticeship, such as "Childhood," "Tales of Sevastopol," and "The Cossacks"; his maturity, when the fresh, keen-sighted realism that characterized his first work took on a deeper, intellectual dimension in his masterpieces *War and Peace* and *Anna Karenina;* and his old age, when his religious conversion seemed to transform a spontaneous artist into a single-minded and almost compulsive moral teacher. But if one remembers the story of the green stick and appreciates its continuing significance in Tolstoy's life, these neat divisions break down. Indeed, after his religious conversion Tolstoy decided that his main task as a writer was to express "the religious perception of his time," and this religious perception illuminated precisely the need for human brotherhood. Thus it is evident that the childhood experience with his brother Nicholas had a mythic value for Tolstoy—that is, it was for him both deeply meaningful and strangely unfathomable, as all myths are—and in his last period, when he devoted himself almost entirely to writing fables and folktales, he was in fact trying to give universal form to a mythic experience which was exquisitely intimate and personal.

This accounts for the way in which his last tales, such as "Ivan the Fool," "Esarhaddon, King of Assyria," and "Emelyan and the Empty Drum," are at once similar to the run of fables and fairy tales yet very much unlike them. The manner of their difference lies in Tolstoy's effort to allegorize and explain the mythic content of his original childhood experience. In most fairy tales, the hero's humility and kindness are the human traits which permit him to overcome the dangers and obstacles in his path and win his just reward; and he is rewarded with wealth or happiness or the princess's hand because he is humble and kind. In Tolstoy's tales, however, the hero's humility and kindness are simply the preconditions for the achievement of greater wisdom and self-awareness, and his reward is never wealth or personal success but rather his ability to conquer, both for himself and others, a new and deeper area of human value and responsibility. Thus, if one believes that a folktale or fable is merely an entertainment, providing the same sort of formal pleasure that one gets from Mallarmé's poetry or abstract painting, then Tolstoy's tales, which above all intend to "prove" the reality and urgency of a whole moral world, can only be criticized as a misuse of the form.

I must admit that I am not at all disturbed by Tolstoy's manhandling of the fabulistic proprieties. One could expect just that when a genius of his particular gifts encounters an ancient form and bends it to his special purposes. The wonder of it is that these stories, despite all the ideological and moral preachments they carry, are yet so successful as sheer stories. Much has been made in recent years of the lacerating conflicts that plagued Tolstoy in his old age. But none of these critics have turned their analytical attention to the fables and folktales. If they had considered them, they would quickly have seen that Tolstoy's realism, the acute and absolute perception which operates so directly and beautifully in his great novels and, at the same time, made it so difficult for him to find an all-embracing intellectual system that would satisfy his heart as well as his head, has here achieved an ideal, well-nigh perfect transfiguration. It is a starkly simple transfiguration, but with all of Tolstoy's essential personal qualities still intact —his straightforwardness, his shrewdness, his incisive intellectual power, his mordant humor. (And it must be said that Ann Dunnigan's translation of the tales for this book is superior to all previous translations because it does deftly capture all these qualities, and particularly the glinting undercurrent of humor.)

Artists can triumph only in their art; in life they undergo the defeats and miseries of the common human lot. It is true that Tolstoy's emotional and intellectual conflicts remained with him to the day of his death, unresolved and perhaps unresolvable. But it is also true that in his last fables and folktales he gave triumphant expression to the bare essentials of his spirit. And I would contend that, viewed in this light, Tolstoy in his old age no longer seems disheartened and death-haunted, a master of words weary of his art, but rather a serene and accomplished sage who knew the value of words and used them with inspired frugality.

I am not trying to unravel Tolstoy's enormous complexity by offering a quaint, fairy-tale view of him. The colossal creator who composed the great novelistic symphonies will not yield up his secret so easily. But the fact remains that side by side with this titan stands the humble, unassuming man who wrote the simple tales. And the simplicity that speaks in these tales is quite palpably not a contrived or affected simplicity, for, as every writer knows, of all literary genres the simple tale is the hardest to fake and the easiest in which to detect the insincere and false. What's more, Tolstoy's simplicity was not a facile achievement. It arose out of a vastly complicated intellectual ferment. Consider: Tolstoy was a rationalist and a desperate God-seeker, a hater of all orthodoxy and a stifled dogmatist, a steadfast believer in the essential goodness and creativity of man and one of the keenest intellects ever to expose man's vices and duplicities. And yet, though pulled in so many divergent directions, Tolstoy somehow managed "to become as a child" and to write the slight, pellucid, sardonic tales that one reads in this book.

There are many explanations, and good ones, of the titanic Tolstoy. There is Maxim Gorky's deeply perceptive memoir, in which he sees Tolstoy as a demonic enchanter, a part of nature itself, an old, sick man sitting by the coast, "the wind blowing the silvery hairs of his beard: he was looking into the distance out to sea, and the little greenish waves rolled up obediently to his feet and fondled them as if they were telling something about themselves to the old magician." There is Thomas Mann's organ-rolling eloquence: "The Homeric, the timeless epic was strong in Tolstoy, as perhaps in no other artist in the world. His work has the epic's long oceanic swell, its majestic monotone; its powerful, astringent freshness and tang, its immortal healthiness and realism." But, strangely enough, few writers have bothered to deal with the simple Tolstoy, the Tolstoy of the fables and folk tales.

They have dealt, it is true, with the Tolstoy whose ideas for the redemption of mankind were so dogmatically and passionately expressed, and for some reason they imagined that by doing so they were also dealing with the Tolstoy I am talking about. They were wrong. In general their oversight was due, I believe, to embarrassment, the sort of embarrassment that often seizes writers and critics when confronted with an elemental fact that cries out for an elemental epithet. For the truth of the matter is that Tolstoy was able to write these tales with such purity and grace because he possessed that Biblical virtue—loving-kindness. It was his supreme virtue, both as a man and as an artist. His biographer Aylmer Maude has given us the best insight into this by his vivid description of Tolstoy as a child. "He was," Maude reports one of Tolstoy's relatives as saying, "like a ray of light. He would come into the room with a happy smile as if he had made a discovery about which he wished to tell everyone." The miracle is that the grown-up Tolstoy somehow retained that virtue. In his great novels it is this quality of openheartedness that makes his characters so alive and astonishingly real. And in preparing to write his fables he gave this emotion unreservedly not to a sensual society matron or a morose, stubborn general but to the young peasant boys whom he had brought together to teach in the school on his estate.

For Tolstoy was perhaps the first proponent of the theory and practice of progressive education. He fervently believed that "to teach and educate a child is impossible and senseless on the simple ground that the child stands nearer than I do, nearer than any adult does, to that ideal of harmony, truth, beauty and goodness to which, in my pride, I wish to lead him." Of course, believing as he did, Tolstoy ran his school in such a manner that he was as much the pupil as the teacher. Eventually this educational experiment was abandoned and later on he revised and modified some of his more extreme views on the subject. But there was one lasting acquisition from all his educational fervor and enthusiasm—a reading primer which Tolstoy labored over long and finally published in 1872, a

few years after he had written *War and Peace*. Among
such books this primer is perhaps unique, for it is the out-
come of the collaboration of a refined genius of language
with the raw genius of the folk, as represented by the
young peasant boys in Tolstoy's school.

In fact, when writing all his folktales, Tolstoy not only
accepted but eagerly sought the corrections and elabora-
tions of the peasants among whom he lived. Although we
have it straight from him that vanity is a driving force in
any writer, it seems that he was capable of holding his own
in check, even of obliterating it, for the sake of a sharp
phrase, an apt example, or a happier turn of speech. One
of the many disciples that Tolstoy's doctrines gathered
about him in his last years tells us how the old man, after
reading his just completed story "Ivan the Fool" to a
group of peasants, asked one of them to repeat it in his
own words. The peasant, who had a remarkable gift for
words, altered the story considerably. But Tolstoy was
delighted by his changes, copied them down rapidly, and
published the story in the new form the peasant had given
it. He explained to his disciple that he always did that; it
was, he said, "the only way to write stories for the people."

It is this last point that has aroused the wrath of so
many critics. They object to the whole notion of "stories
written for the people." They protest against the didactic,
preaching note. They attack the moralistic tone that dis-
torts the variety and fullness of life in order to promul-
gate a message, however good or reasonable. They con-
trast the early Tolstoy who wrote the masterpieces with the
late, dogmatic Tolstoy who, they say, had withered into
a doctrinaire of his own feelings and views. I do not intend
to argue with them. This book will either be enjoyed for its
own sake and prove me right in holding that the Tolstoy
of the fables is as precious to us as the Tolstoy of the
masterpieces, or it will fail to delight readers and therefore
prove me wrong.

I can only hope that what happened to G. K. Chesterton
happens to all the people who read this book. Chesterton,
a volatile man and a vehement preacher, set out to refute
the "preaching" Tolstoy but ended with: "The real dis-
tinction between the ethics of high art and the ethics of
manufactured and didactic art lies in the simple fact that

the bad fable has a moral, while the good fable is a moral.
And the real moral of Tolstoy comes out constantly . . . ,
the great moral which lies at the heart of all his work, of
which he is probably unconscious. . . . It is the curious
cold white light of morning that shines over all the tales,
the folklore simplicity with which 'a man and a woman'
are spoken of without further clarification, the love—one
might almost say the lust—for the qualities of brute ma-
terials, the hardness of wood, and the softness of mud, the
ingrained belief in a certain kind of ancient kindliness
sitting beside the very cradle of the race of man."

Raymond Rosenthal

FABLES
AND
FAIRY TALES

THE PEASANT
AND THE CUCUMBERS

A peasant once went to a vegetable garden to steal cucumbers.

"I'll carry off this sack of cucumbers," he thought, "and with the money I get for them I'll buy a hen. The hen will lay eggs, she will sit on them and hatch a brood of chicks, and I'll feed the chicks till they grow, then I'll sell them and buy a suckling pig. I'll feed the suckling pig till it grows into a sow, I'll breed her, she'll have a litter of pigs, and I'll sell them. With the money I get for the pigs I'll buy a mare. She will foal, I'll feed the foals till they grow, then I'll sell them. With the money I get for the foals I'll buy a house with a garden. I'll plant cucumbers in the garden, and I won't let anyone steal them—I'll keep guard over them. I'll hire a strong watchman, and from time to time I'll go out to the garden and shout: 'Hey, you! Take care!' "

The peasant was so carried away by his thoughts that he completely forgot he was in someone else's garden, and he shouted at the top of his voice.

The watchman heard him and came running out. He caught the peasant and gave him a good beating.

(First Reader)
1872

THE KING
AND THE SHIRT

A king once fell ill.

"I will give half my kingdom to the man who can cure me," he said.

All his wise men gathered together to decide how the king could be cured. But no one knew. Only one of the wise men said what he thought would cure the king.

"If you can find a happy man, take his shirt, put it on the king—and the king will be cured."

The king sent his emissaries to search for a happy man. They traveled far and wide throughout his whole kingdom, but they could not find a happy man. There was no one who was completely satisfied: if a man was rich he was ailing; if he was healthy he was poor; if he was rich and healthy he had a bad wife; or if he had children they were bad—everyone had something to complain of.

Finally, late one night, the king's son was passing by a poor little hut and he heard someone say:

"Now, God be praised, I have finished my work, I have eaten my fill, and I can lie down and sleep! What more could I want?"

The king's son rejoiced and gave orders that the man's shirt be taken and carried to the king, and that the man be given as much money as he wanted.

The emissaries went in to take off the man's shirt, but the happy man was so poor that he had no shirt.

(Fourth Reader)
1872

PETER THE FIRST
AND THE PEASANT

Tsar Peter one day came upon a peasant in the forest.
The peasant was cutting wood.

"God's help, peasant!" said the tsar.

"It's God's help that I need," replied the peasant.

"Is your family a large one?" inquired the tsar.

"I have two sons and two daughters."

"Well, that is not a large family. What do you do with
your money?"

"I divide my money into three parts," said the peasant.
"The first part goes to pay a debt; the second part I give
on loan; and the third part I throw away."

The tsar thought about this, but he did not understand
what it meant.

"I pay a debt," said the peasant, "by feeding my par-
ents; I give a loan by feeding my sons; and I throw away
money by breeding daughters."

"You have a sharp wit, old man," said the tsar. "Now
lead me out of the forest to the field, I have lost my way."

"Find the road yourself," replied the peasant. "Go
straight, then turn right, then left, then right again."

"I don't understand such directions," said the tsar. "You guide me."

"I have no time, sir, to guide you. For us peasants, time is worth money."

"Well, if time is worth money, I shall pay you."

"Oh, if you are going to pay me, let's go!"

They climbed into the gig and drove off.

"Peasant, tell me, have you ever gone far from here?"

"Oh, yes, I've been here and there."

"And have you ever seen the tsar?"

"I have not seen the tsar, but I should like to have a look at him."

"When we come to the field, you will see the tsar."

"And how will I know him?"

"Everyone will be bareheaded except the tsar; he alone will keep on his hat."

They came to the field, and when the people saw the tsar they all took off their hats. The peasant stared intently, but he was unable to find the tsar.

"But where is the tsar?" he asked.

And Peter the First said to him: "You and I seem to be the only ones who are wearing hats—one of us must be the tsar."

(Second Reader)
1872

THE KING
AND THE FALCON

A certain king once went hunting. He loosed his favorite falcon to catch a hare and galloped after him.

The falcon caught the hare. The king took it from him and then began to look for water in order to quench his thirst. He found water on a hillside, but it trickled in drops. He took a cup from his saddle and placed it under the water. The water fell drop by drop. When the cup was full, the king raised it to his mouth and was about to drink.

Suddenly the falcon on his wrist roused himself, beat his wings, and splashed the water out of the cup. The king again placed the cup under the water. He waited a long time until it was filled to the brim. Once more, as he started to raise it to his mouth, the falcon fluttered his wings and spilled the water.

When the king filled the cup for the third time and was about to raise it to his lips, the falcon again spilled it. The king grew angry, and he took up a stone and struck the falcon with all his might and killed him.

Then the king's servants rode up to him, and one of

them ran up the hill to the spring, where there was more water and the cup could be filled more rapidly. He returned with an empty cup and said:

"One cannot drink that water: there is a serpent in the spring, and it has discharged its venom into the water. If you had drunk it you would have died."

"How badly I have repaid the falcon," said the king. "He saved my life and I killed him."

(Third Reader)
1872

THE MOUSE
WHO LIVED UNDER THE GRANARY

There was once a mouse who lived under a granary. And in the floor of the granary there was a little hole through which the grain sifted.

Thus the mouse lived well. He wanted to show off before his friends, so he gnawed at the hole until it was larger, and then invited the other mice to be his guests.

"Come to my place," he said to them, "and I'll treat everyone. There'll be food for all."

When his guests arrived he led them to the hole only to find that it was no longer there.

The large hole had attracted the peasant's notice, and he had stopped it up.

(Second Reader)
1872

THE WOLF
AND
THE OLD WOMAN

A hungry wolf went hunting for food. In a hut at the edge of the village a little boy was crying, and the wolf overheard an old

woman saying to him: "If you don't stop crying I'll give you to the wolf!" The wolf went no farther. He sat down and waited for the little boy to be given to him.

Night came and he was still waiting. Suddenly he heard the old woman say:

"Don't cry, little one, I won't give you to the wolf. Just let that old wolf come, and we'll kill him!"

"There are evidently people here who say one thing and do another," thought the wolf. And he got up and left the village.

(First Reader)
1872

THE PEASANT
AND
THE PRECIOUS STONE

A peasant one day found a precious stone, and he took it to the tsar. When he arrived at court he asked the servants to tell him how he could find the tsar. One of them asked him why he wanted to see the tsar, and when the peasant told him he said:

"Very well, I will take you to him, but only if you promise to give me half of whatever he gives you."

The peasant promised, and the servant took him to the tsar.

The tsar took the precious stone from the peasant and said:

"What shall I give you as a reward, peasant?"

"Give me fifty strokes of the lash; that is the only reward I desire. And since your servant and I have agreed to divide the reward equally, twenty-five are for him."

The tsar laughed and gave the peasant a thousand rubles, and he sent the servant away.

(Primer)
1872

THE DUCK
AND THE MOON

A duck was once swimming along the river looking for fish. The whole day passed without her finding a single one.

When night came she saw the moon reflected on the water, and thinking it was a fish she dove down to catch it. The other ducks saw her and they all made fun of her.

From that day the duck was so ashamed and so timid that even when she did see a fish under water she would not try to catch it, and before long she died of hunger.

(Second Reader)
1872

THE LEARNED SON

A son once returned from the city to his father, who lived in the country.

"We're mowing today," said the father. "Take a rake and come and help me."

But the son did not want to work, so he said: "I am a scholar, and I have forgotten all those peasant words. What is a rake?"

As he walked across the yard he stepped on a rake that was lying in his way and it struck him on the forehead. He suddenly seemed to recall what a rake was, and, clutching his head he cried: "What fool left a rake lying here?"

(First Reader)
1872

EQUAL INHERITANCE

A certain merchant had two sons. The elder son was his favorite, and he intended to leave all his wealth to him when he died. The mother felt sorry for her younger son, and she asked her husband not to tell the boy of his intention. She hoped to find some way of making her sons equal. The merchant heeded her wish and did not make known his decision.

One day the mother was sitting at the window weeping. A pilgrim approached the window and asked her why she was weeping.

"How can I help weeping?" she said. "There is no difference between my two sons, but their father wishes to leave everything to one and nothing to the other. I have asked him not to tell them of his decision until I have thought of some way of helping the younger. But I have no money of my own, and I do not know what to do in my misery."

Then the pilgrim said to her:

"There is help for your trouble: tell your sons that the elder will receive the entire inheritance, and that the younger will receive nothing; then they will be equal."

The younger son, on learning that he would inherit nothing, went to another land, where he served his apprenticeship and learned a trade. The elder son lived at home and learned nothing, knowing that someday he would be rich.

When the father died, the elder son did not know how to do anything and spent all his inheritance, while the younger son, who had learned how to make money in a foreign country, became rich.

(Second Reader)
1872

THE RAVEN
AND HIS YOUNG

The raven built his nest on an island, and when his young were hatched he began carrying them from the island to the mainland. He took the first one up in his claws and flew with him across the sea.

When he reached the middle of the ocean he grew tired, and his wings beat more slowly.

"Now I am strong and he is weak, and I am carrying him across the sea," he thought, "but when he grows great and powerful and I am old and weak, will he remember my toil and carry me from one place to another?" And the old raven asked the young one: "When I am weak and you are strong, will you carry me? Tell me the truth!"

The young raven was afraid that his father might drop him into the ocean, and he said: "I will!"

But the old raven did not believe his son, and he opened his claws and let him fall. He dropped like a lump and drowned in the sea. The old raven flew back to his island.

Then he took his second son in his claws and flew with him across the sea. Again he grew tired, and again he asked his son whether he would carry him from place to place when he was old. The young raven, afraid of being dropped into the ocean, said: "I will!"

The father did not believe this son either, and he let him fall into the sea.

When the old raven flew back to his nest there remained only one young raven. He took his last son and flew with him across the sea. When he came to the middle of the ocean and grew tired he asked: "Will you feed me and carry me from place to place in my old age?"

"No, I will not," the young raven replied.

"Why not?" asked the father.

"When you are old and I am grown I shall have my own nest and my own young to feed and carry."

"He speaks the truth," thought the old raven. "I shall exert myself and carry him across the sea."

And the old raven did not drop the young one, but beat his wings with his last remaining strength in order to carry him to the mainland so that he could build his nest and raise his young.

(Fourth Reader)
1872

THREE ROLLS
AND A PRETZEL

Feeling hungry one day, a peasant bought himself a large roll and ate it. But he was still hungry, so he bought another roll and ate it. Still hungry, he bought a third roll and ate it. When the three rolls failed to satisfy his hunger, he bought some pretzels. After eating one pretzel he no longer felt hungry.

Suddenly he clapped his hand to his head and cried:

"What a fool I am! Why did I waste all those rolls? I ought to have eaten a pretzel in the first place!"

(Second Reader)
1872

THE FALCON
AND THE COCK

The falcon was accustomed to his master and used to go and sit on his wrist when he was called, while the cock, when approached, ran away with a cry.

"You cocks are lacking in gratitude," said the falcon. "It is clear that you are a servile breed: you never go to your masters unless you are hungry. Not at all like us wild birds: we have great strength and can fly faster than anyone, but we don't run from people—we go to them of our own free will when we are called. We don't forget that they feed us."

"You don't run from people," replied the cock, "because you have never seen roasted falcon, while we, from time to time, do see roasted chicken."

(Second Reader)
1872

THE GNAT
AND THE LION

A gnat flew up to a lion and said:
"You think you're stronger than I am, don't you? Well, you are quite wrong! What sort of strength have you got? You scratch with your claws and gnaw with your teeth,

the way peasant women fight with their husbands. I'm stronger than you are. Come on, let's fight!"

And sounding his trumpet, the gnat began to sting the lion on his bare nose and cheeks. The lion struck out with his paws, tearing and clawing his face till it bled and he was exhausted.

Trumpeting with joy, the gnat flew away. But it was not long before he became entangled in a spider's web, and the spider started sucking his blood.

"I overpowered the lion, strongest of beasts," thought the gnat, "and now I am destroyed by a miserable spider!"

(Third Reader)
1872

THE
GOLDEN-HAIRED
PRINCESS

In India there was once a golden-haired princess who had a wicked stepmother. The stepmother conceived a hatred for her stepdaughter and persuaded the king to banish her to the desert. The princess was led far into the desert and abandoned there. On the fifth day she returned to her father riding on the back of a lion.

The stepmother then persuaded the king to banish the golden-haired princess to a mountain wilderness where nothing but vultures lived. On the fourth day the vultures carried her back to her home.

The stepmother next banished the princess to an island in the middle of the sea. Some fishermen caught sight of the golden-haired princess, took her into their boat, and on the sixth day brought her back to the king.

The stepmother then had a deep well dug in the court-yard, lowered the princess into it, and covered her with earth.

After six days a light began to shine from the place where the princess had been buried, and when the king gave orders for the ground to be dug up, the golden-haired princess was found.

Then the stepmother commanded that the log of a mul-berry tree be hollowed out, and she placed the princess in it and put it out to sea.

On the eighth day the sea brought the golden-haired princess to the land of Japan. When the Japanese lifted her out of the hollow tree trunk, she was alive!

But as soon as she set foot on the shore she died and was transformed into a silkworm.

The silkworm crawled up onto the mulberry tree and began to eat the leaves. When it had grown, all at once it appeared to be dead: it neither ate nor moved.

On the fifth day, the same time it took for the lion to carry the princess out of the desert, the worm came to life and again began to eat the leaves.

And after growing, the worm again died. On the fourth day, the same time it took for the vultures to bring the princess back, the worm came to life and again began to eat.

And again it died, and came back to life in the same number of days it took for the fishermen's boat to bring the princess home.

It died a fourth time, and came to life on the sixth day, the day on which the princess had been dug out of the well.

Once more, for the last time, it died; and on the eighth day, which was the day the princess had arrived in Japan, the worm came to life in a golden, silken chrysalis. Out of the chrysalis flew a butterfly. The butterfly laid her eggs, and from the eggs were hatched worms, which began to multiply throughout Japan.

Five times the worm fell ino a sleep, and five times came back to life.

The Japanese breed many silkworms, and they make a great deal of silk. And the worm's first sleep is called the sleep of the lion; and the second—the sleep of the vulture; the third—the sleep of the boat; the fourth—the sleep of the courtyard; and the fifth—the sleep of the log.

(Second Reader)
1872

BIRDS IN A NET

A hunter once set his net by a lake and caught a great many birds. But the birds were large, and they lifted the net and flew off with it. The hunter began to run after it when a peasant saw him and said:

"Where are you going? Do you think you can catch those birds on foot?"

"If there were only one bird in the net, I would not be able to catch it," said the hunter, "but I'll catch these."

And that is just what happened.

When evening came all the birds in the net began to pull in different directions, each heading for his own nest: one toward the forest, another toward the swamp, a third toward the field. Before long they all fell to earth in the net, and the hunter gathered them up.

(Third Reader)
1872

THE HEDGEHOG
AND THE HARE

One day the hare met the hedgehog and he said: "You wouldn't be so bad, hedgehog, except that your legs are crooked, and you stumble."

The hedgehog grew angry and said: "What are you laughing at? My crooked legs can run faster than your straight ones. Just let me go home for a moment, and then you and I shall run a race!"

The hedgehog went home and said to his wife: "I had an argument with the hare and we're going to run a race."

The hedgehog's wife said: "You must be out of your mind! How can you run a race with the hare? His legs are nimble, while yours are crooked and slow!"

"His legs may be nimble," replied the hedgehog, "but my wits are nimble. You have only to do as I tell you. Now, let us go to the field."

They went to the plowed field where the hare was waiting.

"You hide at this end of the furrow," said the hedgehog to his wife. "The hare and I will start from the other end. As soon as he begins to run I'll turn around and go back. When he reaches this end you come out and say: 'I've

46

been waiting here a long time for you!' He can't tell one of us from the other, and he'll think you are me."

The hedgehog's wife hid in the furrow, and the hare and the hedgehog started their race from the other end.

As soon as the hare began to run, the hedgehog turned back and hid in the furrow. When the hare reached the other end, what did he see?—There sat the hedgehog's wife!

"I've been waiting for you a long time!" she said.

"What a miracle!" thought the hare, who could not tell her from her husband. "How could he have outrun me?"

"Come," he said aloud, "let's run again!"

"All right!"

The hare set off, and when he arrived at the other end, what did he see?—There sat the hedgehog!

"Well, brother," he said, "at last you're here! I've been waiting a long time!"

"What a miracle!" thought the hare. "No matter how fast I run, he always outruns me!"

"Come," he said, "let us run again, and this time you won't beat me!"

"All right!" said the hedgehog.

The hare hopped away as fast as he could, but again the hedgehog sat waiting at the end of the furrow.

And thus the hare continued hopping from one end of the furrow to the other until he was exhausted.

He finally gave up and said that henceforth he would never argue again.

(Second Reader)
1872

THE TWO MERCHANTS

A poor merchant was going on a journey and he left all his ironware in the care of a rich merchant. On his return he went to the rich merchant and asked for his goods.

The rich merchant had sold everything, and he tried to justify himself by saying: "An unfortunate thing happened to your ironware."

"And what is that?"

"I put it in the granary and the mice got at it. They riddled it all to bits. I myself saw them gnawing at it. If you don't believe me, come and see for yourself."

The poor merchant did not argue. "Why should I go and see?" he said. "I believe you. I know that mice always gnaw on iron. Good-bye."

And the poor merchant went away.

On the street he saw a little boy playing; he was the son of the rich merchant. Caressing the little boy, he took him by the hand and led him home with him.

The next day the rich merchant met the poor merchant and told him of his great sorrow: his son was lost. And he asked the poor merchant if he had seen or heard anything of him.

"Indeed, I saw him. Just as I was leaving your house yesterday a hawk flew down, seized your little boy, and carried him off."

The rich merchant grew angry and said: "You ought to be ashamed of making fun of me! Do you think anyone would believe that a hawk could carry off a child?"

"I am not making fun of you. Why is it so surprising that a hawk carries off a child when mice devour a hundred poods of iron? Anything can happen."

Then the rich merchant understood. "The mice didn't eat your iron," he said. "I sold it. I shall give you twice what I got for it."

"Well, in that case, the hawk didn't carry off your son, and I shall give him back to you."

(First Reader)
1872

THE MERCHANT
AND THE PURSE

A rich merchant once lost his purse, and he let it be known that the purse contained two thousand rubles, half of which he would give to whoever found it.

A workman found the purse and brought it to the merchant. Now the merchant began to feel that it would be a pity to give up

the money he had promised, so he decided to pretend that, besides the money, there had been a precious stone in the purse.

"I will not give you the money," he said. "There was a precious stone in the purse. Give back the stone, and then I will give you the thousand rubles."

The workman went to court, and the judge reasoned thus:

"You say that your purse contained two thousand rubles and a precious stone," he said to the merchant. "There is no precious stone in this purse, so it cannot be yours. Let the workman keep the purse until its owner is found; and you, make known your loss, and perhaps your purse will be found."

The merchant ceased arguing and gave the workman the thousand rubles.

(Primer)
1872

HOW THE PEASANT
DIVIDED THE GEESE

A poor peasant once found himself without grain, and he conceived the idea of going to his landlord and asking for some. To avoid going empty-handed, he caught a goose, roasted it, and took it with him.

The landlord accepted the goose and said to the peasant: "Thank you, peasant, for the goose. But I don't know how we are going to divide it. You see, I have a wife, two sons, and two daughters. How can we divide the goose without offending anyone?"

"I'll divide it," said the peasant.

He took up a knife, cut off the goose's head, and gave it to the landlord.

"You are the head of the house," he said, "that is for you."

Then he cut off the tail and gave it to the landlord's wife.

"You stay behind looking after the household, that is for you."

Then he cut off the legs and gave them to the two sons.

"You'll soon be following in your father's footsteps—those are for you."

And to the daughters he gave the two wings.

"You'll soon be flying away from your home—those are for you."

And he took all the rest for himself.

The landlord laughed and gave the peasant not only the grain he had asked for but money as well.

Now a rich peasant, hearing that the poor peasant had been given both money and grain, roasted five geese and took them to the landlord.

"Thank you for the geese," said the landlord. "But, you see, I have a wife, and two sons, and two daughters—we are six in all. How shall I divide the five geese into six equal parts?"

The rich peasant thought and thought, but he could not figure out a way.

The landlord sent for the poor peasant and asked him to divide the geese. The poor peasant took one of the geese and handed it to the landlord and his wife.

"There you are," he said, "that makes three of you."

He gave one of the geese to the two sons.

"And that makes three of you."

And he gave one to the two daughters.

"And three of you."

He took the two remaining geese for himself and said: "And three of us. Now we are all even."

The landlord laughed and again gave the poor peasant money and grain, but he drove the rich peasant away.

(Third Reader)
1872

THE SNAKE

A certain woman once had a daughter named Masha. One day Masha went swimming with her friends. The girls took off their smocks, placed them on the bank, and jumped into the water.

A big snake crawled out of the water and coiled up on Masha's smock. Soon the girls came out of the water, put

on their clothes, and ran home. When Masha went to pick up her smock and saw the large snake lying on it, she took up a stick and was about to drive him away, but the snake lifted his head and spoke to her in a gruff human voice.

"Masha, Masha, promise that you will marry me!"

Masha burst into tears and said: "Give me my smock, and I will do anything!"

"Will you marry me?"

"I will."

The snake crawled off her smock and slipped back into the water.

Masha dressed and ran home. When she got home she said to her mother: "Mama, a big snake was lying on my smock, and he said: 'Marry me, or I won't give it back to you.' And I promised him I would."

Her mother laughed and said: "You had a dream."

A week later a whole swarm of snakes crawled up to Masha's house. When she saw them she grew frightened and said:

"Mama, the snakes have come for me!"

At first her mother did not believe her, but when she saw all the snakes she too became frightened. She locked both the gate and the door into the house. The snakes crawled under the gate and into the entry, but they were unable to get into the house. So they crawled back again, rolled themselves up into a big ball, and threw themselves at the window. They broke the glass and fell in onto the floor. They crawled all over the benches and tables and up onto the stove, where Masha was hiding in a corner. They soon found her, pulled her down, and led her away to the water.

The mother cried and ran after them, but she could not overtake them, and they plunged into the water with Masha.

The mother wept for her daughter, thinking that she was now dead.

One day, as she sat at the window gazing into the street, she suddenly saw Masha coming toward her, leading a little boy by the hand and carrying a baby girl. The mother was overjoyed. She kissed her daughter and began asking her where she had been and whose children these were. Masha said the children were hers, that she had married

the snake and now lived with him in his watery kingdom. When the mother asked her daughter whether she liked living there Masha told her she liked it much better than living on land.

The mother asked her to remain with her, but Masha refused. She said she had promised her husband that she would come back to him.

"And how are you going to return to your home?" asked the mother.

"I shall go to the water's edge and call: 'Osip, Osip, come out and get me!' And he will come to the bank and take me away."

"Very well," said the mother, "only spend the night here with me."

When Masha fell asleep her mother took a hatchet and went down to the water.

"Osip, Osip," she called, "come out!"

The snake swam up to the shore. The mother struck him with the hatchet and cut off his head, and the water turned red with his blood.

When the mother got home her daughter woke up and said:

"I'm going home now, Mama. I'm beginning to feel lonely here." She picked up her little daughter, took her son by the hand, and went away.

When she came to the water she called: "Osip, Osip, come to me!"

But no one came. Then she looked at the water and saw that it was all red, with the head of a snake floating on it.

Masha kissed her son and her daughter and said to them:

"You have no father, and you will have no mother. You, little daughter, be a baby swallow and fly over the water; and you, my little son, be a young nightingale and sing at twilight; and I shall be a cuckoo and cry for my husband who has been slain."

And they all flew away in different directions.

(Second Reader)
1872

A JUST JUDGE

An Algerian king named Bauakas wanted to find out whether or not it was true, as he had been told, that in one of his cities there lived a just judge who could instantly discern the truth, and from whom no rogue was ever able to conceal himself. Bauakas exchanged clothes with a merchant and went on horseback to the city where the judge lived.

At the entrance to the city a cripple approached the king and begged alms of him. Bauakas gave him money and was about to continue on his way, but the cripple clung to his clothing.

"What do you wish?" asked the king. "Haven't I given you money?"

"You gave me alms," said the cripple, "now grant me one favor. Let me ride with you as far as the city square, otherwise the horses and camels may trample me."

Bauakas sat the cripple behind him on the horse and took him as far as the city square. There he halted his horse, but the cripple refused to dismount.

"We have arrived at the square, why don't you get off?" asked Bauakas.

"Why should I?" the beggar replied. "This horse belongs to me. If you are unwilling to return it, we shall have to go to court."

Hearing their quarrel, people gathered around them shouting:

"Go to the judge! He will decide between you!"

Bauakas and the cripple went to the judge. There were others in court, and the judge called upon each one in turn. Before he came to Bauakas and the cripple he heard a scholar and a peasant. They had come to court over a woman: the peasant said she was his wife, and the scholar said she was his. The judge heard them both, remained silent for a moment, and then said:

"Leave the woman here with me, and come back tomorrow."

When they had gone, a butcher and an oil merchant came before the judge. The butcher was covered with blood, and the oil merchant with oil. In his hand the butcher held some money, and the oil merchant held onto the butcher's hand.

"I was buying oil from this man," the butcher said, "and when I took out my purse to pay him, he seized me by the hand and tried to take all my money away from me. That is why we have come to you—I holding onto my purse, and he holding onto my hand. But the money is mine, and he is a thief."

Then the oil merchant spoke. "That is not true," he said. "The butcher came to me to buy oil, and after I had poured him a full jug, he asked me to change a gold piece for him. When I took out my money and placed it upon a bench, he seized it and tried to run off. I caught him by the hand, as you see, and brought him here to you."

The judge remained silent for a moment, then said: "Leave the money here with me, and come back tomorrow."

When his turn came, Bauakas told what had happened. The judge listened to him, and then asked the beggar to speak.

"All that he said is untrue," said the beggar. "He was sitting on the ground, and as I rode through the city he asked me to let him ride with me. I sat him behind me on my horse and took him where he wanted to go. But when we got there he refused to get off and said that the horse was his, which is not true."

The judge thought for a moment, then said: "Leave the horse here with me, and come back tomorrow."

The following day many people gathered in court to hear the judge's decisions.

First came the scholar and the peasant.

"Take your wife," the judge said to the scholar, "and the peasant shall be given fifty strokes of the lash."

The scholar took his wife, and the peasant was given his punishment.

Then the judge called the butcher.

"The money is yours," he said to him. And pointing to the oil merchant he said: "Give him fifty strokes of the lash."

He next called Bauakas and the cripple.

"Would you be able to recognize your horse among twenty others?" he asked Bauakas.

"I would," he replied.

"And you?" he asked the cripple.

"I would," said the cripple.

"Come with me," the judge said to Bauakas.

They went to the stable. Bauakas instantly pointed out his horse among the twenty others. Then the judge called the cripple to the stable and told him to point out the horse. The cripple recognized the horse and pointed to it. The judge then returned to his seat.

"Take the horse, it is yours," he said to Bauakas. "Give the beggar fifty strokes of the lash."

When the judge left the court and went home, Bauakas followed him.

"What do you want?" asked the judge. "Are you not satisfied with my decision?"

"I am satisfied," said Bauakas. "But I should like to learn how you knew that the woman was the wife of the scholar, that the money belonged to the butcher, and that the horse was mine and not the beggar's."

"This is how I knew about the woman: in the morning I sent for her and said: 'Please fill my inkwell.' She took the inkwell, washed it quickly and deftly, and filled it with ink; therefore it was work she was accustomed to. If she had been the wife of the peasant she would not have known how to do it. This showed me that the scholar was telling the truth.

"And this is how I knew about the money: I put it into a cup full of water, and in the morning I looked to see if any oil had risen to the surface. If the money had belonged to the oil merchant it would have been soiled by his oily

hands. There was no oil on the water; therefore, the butcher was telling the truth.

"It was more difficult to find out about the horse. The cripple recognized it among twenty others, even as you did. However, I did not take you both to the stable to see which of you knew the horse, but to see which of you the horse knew. When you approached it, it turned its head and stretched its neck toward you; but when the cripple touched it, it laid back its ears and lifted one hoof. Therefore I knew that you were the horse's real master."

Then Bauakas said to the judge: "I am not a merchant, but King Bauakas. I came here in order to see if what is said of you is true. I see now that you are a wise judge. Ask whatever you wish of me, and you shall have it as a reward."

"I need no reward," replied the judge. "I am content that my king has praised me."

(Third Reader)
1872

THE TWO BROTHERS

Two brothers set out on a journey together. At noon
they lay down in a forest to rest. When they woke up they
saw a stone lying next to them. There was something written on the stone, and they tried to make out what it was.

"Whoever finds this stone," they read, "let him go
straight into the forest at sunrise. In the forest a river will
appear; let him swim across the river to the other side.
There he will find a she-bear and her cubs. Let him take
the cubs from her and run up the mountain with them,
without once looking back. On the top of the mountain he
will see a house, and in that house will he find happiness."

When they had read what was written on the stone, the
younger brother said:

"Let us go together. We can swim across the river, carry
off the bear cubs, take them to the house on the mountain,
and together find happiness."

"I am not going into the forest after bear cubs," said the
elder brother, "and I advise you not to go. In the first
place, no one can know whether what is written on this
stone is the truth—perhaps it was written in jest. It is even
possible that we have not read it correctly. In the second
place, even if what is written here is the truth—suppose

we go into the forest and night comes, and we cannot find the river. We shall be lost. And if we do find the river, how are we going to swim across it? It may be broad and swift. In the third place, even if we swim across the river, do you think it is an easy thing to take her cubs away from a she-bear? She will seize us, and, instead of finding happiness, we shall perish, and all for nothing. In the fourth place, even if we succeeded in carrying off the bear cubs, we could not run up a mountain without stopping to rest. And, most important of all, the stone does not tell us what kind of happiness we should find in that house. It may be that the happiness awaiting us there is not at all the sort of happiness we would want."

"In my opinion," said the younger brother, "you are wrong. What is written on the stone could not have been put there without reason. And it is all perfectly clear. In the first place, no harm will come to us if we try. In the second place, if we do not go, someone else will read the inscription on the stone and find happiness, and we shall have lost it all. In the third place: if you do not make an effort and try hard, nothing in the world will succeed. In the fourth place: I should not want it thought that I was afraid of anything."

The elder brother answered him by saying: "The proverb says: 'In seeking great happiness small pleasures may be lost.' And also: 'A bird in the hand is worth two in the bush.'"

The younger brother replied: "I have heard: 'He who is afraid of the leaves must not go into the forest.' And also: 'Beneath a stone no water flows.'"

Then the younger brother set off, and the elder remained behind.

No sooner had the younger brother gone into the forest than he found the river, swam across it, and there on the other side was the she-bear, fast asleep. He took her cubs, and ran up the mountain without looking back. When he reached the top of the mountain the people came out to meet him with a carriage to take him into the city, where they made him their king.

He ruled for five years. In the sixth year, another king, who was stronger than he, waged war against him. The city was conquered, and he was driven out.

Again the younger brother became a wanderer, and he arrived one day at the house of the elder brother. The elder brother was living in a village and had grown neither rich nor poor. The two brothers rejoiced at seeing each other, and at once began telling of all that had happened to them.

"You see," said the elder brother, "I was right. Here I have lived quietly and well, while you, though you may have been a king, have seen a great deal of trouble."

"I do not regret having gone into the forest and up the mountain," replied the younger brother. "I may have nothing now, but I shall always have something to remember, while you have no memories at all."

(Second Reader)
1872

HOW THE IMP
MADE AMENDS FOR
THE CRUST OF BREAD

A poor peasant, going out to plow before breakfast, took with him a crust of bread. He set out the plow, took off his coat, wrapped the crust in it and put it under a bush.

When his horse grew tired and he began to feel hungry, he rested the plow, unharnessed the horse, and went to get his breakfast from under the bush.

He took up his coat—no bread! He looked and he looked, turning the coat inside out and shaking it—but no bread! The peasant was bewildered.

"That's strange!" he said to himself. "I haven't seen anyone, yet someone has taken my crust!"

While the peasant was plowing, an imp had come and stolen the crust of bread, and was now sitting behind the bush waiting to hear the peasant swear and call on the devil—himself.

The peasant was downcast. "Oh, well," he said, "I shan't die of hunger. Whoever took it probably needed it. May it do him good!"

And he went to the well, drank some water, and rested.

The imp was disconcerted by his failure to lead the peasant into sin, and he went to report to the Big Devil.

He appeared to the Big One and told him how he had taken the crust, and how the peasant, instead of cursing, had said: "May it do him good!"

The Big Devil was angry.

"The peasant got the upper hand in this business, and it's your own fault—you made a mess of it! If the peasants, and then their women after them, take to that sort of thing, our life won't be worth living. The matter cannot be left like that! You go back to that peasant and make amends for what you have done. If within three years you haven't got the upper hand with him, I'll dip you in holy water!"

The imp was frightened. He scampered back to earth and tried to figure out how to redeem his mistake. He thought and he thought, and he finally conceived of a plan. He transformed himself into a laborer and hired himself out to the poor peasant.

It was a dry summer and he taught the peasant to sow grain in a marsh. The peasant followed his laborer's advice, and when the crops of the other peasants were scorched by the sun, his grain grew thick, tall, and full-eared. He not only had enough to last him the year but much more besides.

The next summer the laborer told the peasant to sow on the hill, and it turned out to be a rainy summer. The grain of the other peasants was beaten down and rotted without ripening, but his crop on the hill was a fine one. He had even more grain left over than before and did not know what to do with it.

The laborer taught the peasant how to mash the grain and distill liquor from it, and when the peasant had made the liquor he began drinking it himself and giving it to others.

Now the imp went back to the Big Devil and boasted about how he had redeemed himself for the crust of bread. The Devil went to see for himself.

When he arrived he found that the peasant had invited his rich neighbors and was treating them. His wife was serving the liquor to the guests, and as she handed it around she stumbled against the table and spilled a glassful.

The peasant became angry and began to abuse her.

"Watch out, you cursed fool! Do you think it's hogwash, bandy-legs, that you pour such good stuff onto the floor?"

The imp nudged the Devil. "Now see how he doesn't grudge his last crust!"

The peasant, still railing at his wife, began serving the drinks himself.

A poor peasant returning from work came in uninvited. He sat down, and seeing that they were all drinking he felt that he too would like a drop after his day's work. He sat on and on, his mouth watering more all the time; but the host offered him nothing.

"I can't be supplying everyone who comes along," he muttered.

This pleased the Big Devil.

"Wait," the imp boasted, "there's more to come!"

The rich peasants drank and their host drank with them. They soon began fawning on one another, bragging, making flattering and oily speeches.

The Big Devil continued to listen, praising the imp for this too. "If drink makes them so foxy that they begin cheating each other, they'll soon be in our hands."

"Wait for what's still to come," said the imp. "Let them have another glass. Now they are like foxes, wagging their

tails and trying to deceive one another, but watch them turn into savage wolves."

The peasants all had another glass and their talk became louder and coarser. Instead of oily speeches they cursed and snarled at each other, finally coming to blows and beating one another black and blue. The host joined in the fight and he too was given a beating.

The Devil looked on, very pleased. "This," he said, "is excellent!"

"Wait for what's still to come!" said the imp. "Let them have another round. Now they're like mad wolves, but give them time—one more glass and they'll be like swine."

After taking another glass the peasants were besotted. They muttered and shouted without knowing why—they were no longer listening to one another.

The party began to break up. Some went alone, some in pairs, some in threes, all staggering down the street. The host went out to see his guests off, fell on his nose in a puddle, and lay there, covered with mud from head to foot and grunting like a hog.

This pleased the Devil still more. "Well," he said, "you've hit upon a fine drink, and have made up for the crust of bread. But, tell me, how is this drink made? First, you must have put fox blood in it: that made the peasants as sly as foxes, and then—wolf's blood: that made them savage as wolves. And you probably finished off with swine's blood: that made them swinish."

"No," said the imp, "that was not the way I did it. All I had to do was to make the peasant grow more grain than he needed. Beast blood is always in man, but as long as he has only as much as he needs, it's not aroused. Before, the peasant didn't grudge his last crust, but as soon as he had a surplus of grain he commenced to have cravings. And I taught him the pleasure of drink. As soon as he began to turn God's good gift into liquor for his own pleasure, the blood of the fox, the wolf, and the swine all rose up in him. If only he continues to drink, he will always be a beast!"

The Devil praised the imp, forgave him for the crust of bread, and promoted him to a higher position.

1886

ESARHADDON,
KING OF ASSYRIA

Esarhaddon, the Assyrian king, had conquered King Lailie's dominion; he ravaged and burned all the cities, drove the inhabitants back to his own country, slaughtered the warriors, and put King Lailie himself into a cage.

One night King Esarhaddon lay in bed thinking how he would put Lailie to death, when all at once he heard a rustling, and opening his eyes he beheld an old man with a long gray beard and gentle eyes.

"Do you wish to kill Lailie?" asked the old man.

"Yes," the king answered, "but I cannot decide by what means to execute him."

"But you are Lailie," the old man said.

"That is not true," replied the king. "I am I, and Lailie is Lailie."

"You and Lailie are one," said the old man. "It only seems to you that you are not Lailie and that Lailie is not you."

"What do you mean—seems?" said the king. "Here I lie on a soft bed, surrounded by my obedient slaves, and tomorrow, as today, I shall feast with my friends; whereas Lailie sits like a bird in a cage, and tomorrow he will be squirming on a stake with his tongue hanging out till he dies, his body torn to pieces by dogs."

"You cannot destroy his life," said the old man.

"And what of the fourteen thousand warriors I killed—with whose bodies I built a tumulus?" asked the king. "I am alive and they are not; therefore I can destroy life."

74

"How do you know they are not alive?"

"Because I do not see them. And, moreover, they were tortured, not I. It was bad for them, but good for me."

"This, too, seems so to you. You tortured yourself, not them."

"I do not understand," said the king.

"Do you want to understand?"

"I do."

"Come here," said the old man, pointing to a font full of water.

Esarhaddon did as the old man bade him.

"Now, as soon as I begin to pour this water over you," said the old man, dipping a jug into the water, "submerge your head."

As he tipped the jug over him, the king submerged his head.

No sooner was his head under water than he felt that he was no longer Esarhaddon, but someone else. And, feeling himself to be that other man, he saw himself lying on a luxurious bed beside a beautiful woman. He had never seen this woman before, but he knew she was his wife. The woman raised herself and said to him:

"My dear husband, Lailie, you were tired by yesterday's work and have slept longer than usual, and I have watched over your rest and have not roused you. But now the princes await you in the great hall. Dress and go out to them."

And Esarhaddon, understanding from these words that he was Lailie, not only felt no surprise, but even wondered that he had not known this before. And he rose and dressed himself and went to the great hall where the princes attended him.

Bowing to the ground the princes greeted Lailie, their king, then rose, and at his command seated themselves before him. The eldest of them began to speak, saying that it was no longer possible to bear the affronts of the wicked King Esarhaddon, and that they must wage war against him. But Lailie did not agree with them, and commanded that emissaries be sent to Esarhaddon to exhort him, and he dismissed the princes. He then appointed eminent men to act as ambassadors, carefully instructing them in what to say to Esarhaddon.

Having finished these matters, Esarhaddon, feeling himself to be Lailie, rode up into the hills to hunt wild asses. The hunt was successful, the king himself killing two asses, and, when he returned home he feasted with his friends while watching his slave girls dance.

The following day, as was his custom, he went to court, where he was awaited by petitioners, litigants, and prisoners brought to trial, and he judged the cases brought before him. When he had finished, he again rode out to his favorite pastime, hunting. And on that day he succeeded in killing an old lioness and capturing her two cubs. After the hunt he again feasted with his friends, diverting himself with music and dancing, after which he spent the night with his beloved wife.

Thus he lived for days and weeks, while waiting for the return of the ambassadors he had sent to that King Esar-

haddon whom he once had been. Only after a month had gone by did they return—and then with their noses and ears cut off.

King Esarhaddon had instructed them to tell Lailie that what had been done to his ambassadors would be done to him too, unless he immediately sent the specified tribute of silver, gold, and cypress wood, and came in person to pay homage to him.

Lailie, formerly Esarhaddon, again called the princes together and took counsel with them. With one accord they declared that instead of waiting for Esarhaddon to attack them they must go to war against him.

The king agreed, and, taking his place at the head of his army, he set out on the campaign. The march lasted seven days. Each day the king rode among his men, inspiring them to valor. On the eighth day they met Esarhaddon's army in a broad valley on the bank of a river. Lailie's warriors fought bravely, but Lailie, formerly Esarhaddon, saw the enemy swarming down from the mountain like ants, overrunning the valley and vanquishing his army, and he sped his chariot into the midst of the battle, slashing and hewing at the enemy. But Lailie's warriors numbered hundreds, while Esarhaddon's were in the thou-

sands. And Lailie felt that he was wounded, and that they had taken him prisoner.

He marched for nine days with the other captives, bound, and surrounded by Esarhaddon's soldiers. On the tenth day he was brought to Nineveh and put into a cage.

Lailie suffered not so much from his wound and hunger as from shame and impotent rage. He felt powerless to avenge himself for all the evil he was suffering. The one thing he could do was to deprive his enemies of the joy of watching his agony, and he firmly resolved to endure courageously and without a murmur all that happened to him.

For twenty days he sat in the cage awaiting execution. He saw his relatives and friends led out to death, and heard their groans; some had their arms and legs cut off, others were flayed alive, but he showed no agitation, no pity, no fear. He saw his beloved wife bound by two eunuchs, and he realized that she was being taken to Esarhaddon as a slave. And this too he bore in silence.

At last two executioners unlocked the door of his cage, and, after tying his arms behind his back with thongs, they led him to the gory execution site. Lailie saw the sharp, bloodstained stake from which the dead body of one of his friends had just been torn, and he realized that this stake had been cleared for his own execution.

They took off his clothes. Lailie was horrified at the gauntness of his once strong and handsome body. The two executioners seized that body by its scrawny thighs, lifted it up, and were about to impale it on the stake.

"Now death, extinction," Lailie thought, and, forgetting his resolution to remain courageously calm to the end, he sobbed and prayed for mercy. But no one listened to him.

"But this cannot be! Surely I am asleep—it is a dream!" And he made an effort to rouse himself, thinking, "I am not Lailie, I am Esarhaddon."

"You are both Lailie and Esarhaddon," he heard a voice saying, and he felt that now his execution was going to begin.

He cried out, at the same instant raising his head from the font. The old man was standing over him, pouring the last drops of water from the jug onto his head.

"Oh, how terribly I have suffered! And how long!" said Esarhaddon.

"Long?" replied the old man. "You have only just dipped your head under water and raised it again. See, all the water has not yet been poured out of the jug. Do you understand?"

Esarhaddon did not reply, but only looked in terror at the old man.

"Do you understand," the old man continued, "that Lailie is you, that the warriors you put to death also were you? And not only the warriors, but the animals you hunted and slew and afterwards devoured at your feasts, they too were you. You thought life dwelt in you alone, but I have drawn aside the veil of delusion, and you have seen that in doing evil to others you have done it to yourself as well. Life is one in everything, and within yourself you manifest but a portion of this one life. And only in that portion that is within you can you make life better or worse, magnify or diminish it. You can make life better within yourself only by destroying the barriers that divide your life from that of other beings, and by regarding others as yourself and loving them. To destroy the life that dwells in others is not within your power. The life that was in those you have slain has not been destroyed: it has merely vanished from before your eyes. You thought to prolong your own life and to shorten the lives of others, but you cannot do this. For life there is neither time nor space. The life of a moment and the life of thousands of years, your life and the lives of all creatures seen and unseen, is one. To destroy life, even to alter it, is impossible, for life alone exists. All else only seems to be."

Having said this, the old man vanished.

The next morning King Esarhaddon commanded that Lailie and all the prisoners be freed and the executions stopped. And on the following day he summoned his son, Ashurbanipal, and gave over the kingdom into his hands. He himself withdrew into the wilderness to meditate on all that he had learned. Later he went as a pilgrim through the towns and villages, preaching to the people that all life is one, and that men do evil only to themselves in desiring to do evil to others.

1903

THE JACKALS
AND THE ELEPHANT

The jackals had devoured all the carrion in the forest, and they now had nothing to eat. One old jackal conceived a plan for getting food. He went to the elephant and said:

"We once had a king, but he became spoiled and would order us to do impossible things. So we have decided to choose another king. Our people have sent me to ask you to be our king. You'll have a good life with us: whatever you command will be done, and we'll honor you in all things. Come to our kingdom."

The elephant agreed to go with the jackal. When the jackal had led him into the swamp and the elephant was stuck in the mud, the jackal then said to him:

"Command me; whatever you order shall be done."

"I command you to pull me out of here," said the elephant.

The jackal laughed. "Take hold of my tail with your trunk," he said, "and I'll pull you out at once."

"Do you think it is possible to pull me out with your tail?" asked the elephant.

"Why did you command me to do it if it's impossible?" said the jackal. "That's why we got rid of the other king, because he gave us impossible orders."

When the elephant lay dead in the swamp, the jackals came and ate him up.

(Second Reader)
1872

THE THREE QUESTIONS

It once occurred to a certain king that if he always knew just when to undertake everything he did, and which were the right and which the wrong people to deal with, and, above all, if he always knew what was the most important thing to do, he would never fail in anything.

Having thus thought, the king proclaimed throughout his realm that he would bestow a large reward on anyone who would teach him *how to know the proper moment for every deed, how to know which were the most essential people, and how not to err in deciding which pursuits were of the greatest importance.*

Learned men began coming to the king, but they all gave different answers to his questions.

In reply to the first question some said that in order to know the right time for every action one must draw up a schedule of days, months, and years, and strictly adhere to it. Only in this way, they said, could everything be done at the proper time.

Others said it was not possible to decide in advance what to do and when to do it; that one must not allow himself to be distracted by vain amusements, but must be attentive to everything that happens and do whatever is required.

A third group said that no matter how attentive the king might be to what was going on, it was impossible for one man rightly to decide the time for every action, and that he ought to have a council of wise men, and act according to their advice.

A fourth group said that there were certain matters which required immediate decision, leaving no time to determine by means of consultation whether or not it was the right time to undertake them. In order to know this, one would have to know in advance what was going to happen, which is something that only a magician can know; therefore, in order to know the right time for every action, one must consult the magicians.

The answers to the second question also varied. Some said that the people the king most needed were his administrators; some said the priests, and some the physicians, while others said the warriors were the most essential.

The answers to the third question, as to what was the most important pursuit, were equally diverse. Some said that science was the most important thing in the world, some said military skill, and others religious worship.

The answers were all different, therefore the king agreed with none of them and rewarded no one.

In order to find the true answers to his questions, he decided to consult a hermit who was famous for his wisdom.

The hermit never left the forest where he lived, and there he received none but simple folk. The king therefore dressed himself as one of the people, and, dismounting before he reached the hermit's dwelling, he left his knights behind and went on alone.

The king found the hermit digging a garden in front of his hut. When he saw the king, the hermit greeted him and immediately returned to his digging. He was thin and frail, and each time he thrust his spade into the ground and turned a little clod of earth, he breathed heavily.

The king approached him and said: "I have come to you, wise hermit, to ask you for the answers to three questions: *How can I know which is the time I ought to heed, not allowing it to slip by only to be regretted later? Who are the most essential people, those to whom I ought to give the greatest attention? And what are the most impor-*

tant pursuits, which therefore ought to be undertaken first?"

The hermit listened to the king, but gave him no answer; he merely spat on his hands and started digging again.

"You have exhausted yourself," the king said. "Give me the spade. I'll work for a while."

"Thanks," said the hermit. He handed him the spade and sat down on the ground.

After digging two beds, the king stopped and repeated his questions. The hermit did not answer, but got up and held out his hand for the spade, saying:

"Now you rest and I'll work."

But the king did not give him the spade; he went on digging.

An hour passed, then another; the sun had begun to sink behind the trees when the king stuck the spade into the ground and said:

"I came to you, wise man, for answers to my questions. If you can give me none, tell me so and I shall return home."

"Here comes someone running," said the hermit. "Let us see who it is."

The king looked around and saw a bearded man running out of the woods. The man held his hands pressed to his stomach and blood flowed from between his fingers. He ran up to the king and fell fainting to the ground, where he lay motionless, weakly moaning.

The king and the hermit opened the man's clothing.

There was a large wound in his stomach. The king washed
it as well as he could and bandaged it with his own hand-
kerchief and the hermit's towel; but the flow of blood did
not abate. Again and again the king removed the bandage
soaked with warm blood, washed it, and rebandaged the
wound.

When the blood at last ceased flowing, the wounded man
revived and asked for water. The king brought fresh water
and gave him a drink.

Meanwhile the sun had set and it grew cool. The king,
with the hermit's help, carried the wounded man into the
hut and laid him on the bed. He closed his eyes and grew
still. The king was so tired from his walk and the work he
had done that he lay down on the threshold and fell asleep.
And he slept so soundly through the short summer night
that when he woke up in the morning it was some time
before he realized where he was and recalled the bearded
stranger lying on the bed, who was now gazing intently at
him with luminous eyes.

"Forgive me," said the bearded man in a faint voice,
when he saw that the king was awake and looking at him.

"I do not know you and have nothing to forgive you,"
replied the king.

"You do not know me, but I know you. I am your
enemy, and I swore to take vengeance on you for killing
my brother and seizing my property. I knew you had come
alone to see the hermit, and I resolved to kill you on your
way back. But when the whole day passed and you did not
return, I left my ambush to seek you out, and came upon
your knights instead. They recognized me, fell upon me,
and wounded me. I escaped from them, but I should have
bled to death if you had not cared for my wound. I intended
to kill you, and you have saved my life. Now, if I live, and
if you wish it, I will serve you as your most faithful slave,
and bid my sons to do the same. Forgive me!"

The king was happy to be so easily reconciled with his
enemy, and he not only forgave him but promised to return
his property and send his own physician and servants to
attend him.

Having taken leave of the wounded man, the king went
out to look for the hermit. Before leaving him he wished
for the last time to ask him to answer his questions. The

hermit was on his knees in the yard sowing seeds in the beds that had been dug the day before.

The king approached him and said: "For the last time, wise man, I ask you to answer my questions."

"But you have already been answered," said the hermit, squatting on his thin calves and looking up at the king who stood before him.

"How have I been answered?" asked the king.

"How?" repeated the hermit. "Had you not taken pity on my weakness yesterday and dug these beds for me, instead of turning back alone, that fellow would have assaulted you, and you would have regretted not staying with me. Therefore, the most important time was when you were digging the beds; I was the most important man; and the most important pursuit was to do good to me. And later, when that man came running to us, the most important time was when you were taking care of him, for if you had not bound up his wound, he would have died without having made peace with you; therefore he was the most important man, and what you did for him was the most important deed. Remember then: there is only one important time—

Now. And it is important because it is the only time we have dominion over ourselves; and the most important man is *he with whom you are,* for no one can know whether or not he will ever have dealings with any other man; and the most important pursuit is *to do good to him,* since it is for that purpose alone that man was sent into this life."

1903

EMELYAN
AND THE EMPTY DRUM

Emelyan lived at his master's, where he worked as a laborer. One day as he was crossing the meadow on his way to work, out hopped a frog in front of him, almost under his foot. No sooner had he stepped over it than he heard a voice calling him from behind. Emelyan glanced back, and there stood a beautiful maiden.

"Emelyan, why don't you marry?" she said to him.

"How can I marry, pretty maid? Here I am with nothing but myself—no one would marry me."

"Take me for a wife!" she said.

Emelyan was enchanted with the maiden.

"Gladly," he said, "but where would we live?"

"What a thing to think of! You have only to work a little more and sleep a little less, and we shall be fed and clothed wherever we are."

"All right, let us marry," he said. "But where shall we go?"

"Let us go to the town."

Emelyan and the maiden set out together, and she led

him to a little hut at the very end of the town. They were married, and there they lived.

Now it happened one day that the tsar was driving out to the country. As he passed the little house, Emelyan's wife came out to look at him. When the tsar saw her he was astonished.

"Where could such a beauty have come from?" he wondered.

He stopped the carriage, called Emelyan's wife to him, and began to question her.

"Who are you?" he asked.

"I am the wife of the peasant Emelyan," she said.

"Why did such a beauty as you marry a peasant? You ought to be married to a tsar."

"Thank you for your kind words," she said, "but a peasant husband is good enough for me."

The tsar talked with her awhile and then drove on. He returned to his palace, but he was unable to get Emelyan's wife out of his mind. All night long he lay awake trying to think of some way to take her away from Emelyan. But he

could think of none, so he sent for his servants and bade them devise a way.

The servants said to the tsar: "Have Emelyan brought here to the palace to work. We'll work him to death, his wife will be left a widow, and then you can take her."

So the tsar sent for Emelyan to work as a yardman at the palace, and to live in the courtyard with his wife.

When the tsar's emissaries came to tell Emelyan, his wife said to him:

"Go, Emelyan, and work there by day; but at night come back to me."

Emelyan went to the palace. When he got there the tsar's steward said to him:

"Why have you come alone, without your wife?"

"Why should I bring my wife? She has a home."

In the tsar's courtyard Emelyan was given enough work for two men. He started his work with no hope of finishing it; but, to his surprise, it was all done before evening. The steward saw that he finished it and gave him four times as much the next day.

When Emelyan got home he found everything swept clean and in order; the oven was heated, the baking and cooking were done, and his wife sat at her weaving, waiting for her husband to come home. She greeted him, laid the table for supper, gave him food and drink, and then asked him about his work.

"It's bad," he said. "They give me tasks that are beyond my strength. They will wear me out with work."

"Do not think about the work," she said. "Look neither before nor behind you to see how much is done or how much remains to be done. Only work, and all will be finished on time."

Emelyan went to bed and slept, and in the morning he went back again. He worked the whole day without once looking back. And lo and behold!—by evening it was all finished, and he was home before dark.

Again and again they increased his work, but Emelyan always finished on time and returned home for the night.

A week passed, and the tsar's servants began to see that they could not wear the peasant out with hard work. They decided to give him tasks that required skill. But this too was of no avail. No matter what he was given to do—

whether carpentry, masonry, or roofing—Emelyan always finished on time and went home to his wife at night.

Another week passed. Then the tsar sent for his servants.

"Do I feed you for nothing?" he said to them. "Two weeks have gone by, and I can't see that you have done anything! You were going to exhaust Emelyan with work; but each day from my window I see him go home singing a song. Are you trying to make a fool of me?"

The tsar's servants began to justify themselves.

"First we tried our best to wear him out with hard work, but nothing is too much for him. He did everything as though sweeping it up with a broom. And he never grew tired! Then we gave him work that required skill, thinking he would not be clever enough to do it. And still we failed to catch him. It's like magic! There's nothing he can't do! Either he or his wife must practice some kind of sorcery. We ourselves are sick of him. Now we are planning to set him a task that he cannot possibly accomplish: to build a cathedral in one day. Send for him, and tell him it must be built across from the palace, and within one day. And if he fails to do it, then you can have his head cut off for disobedience."

The tsar sent for Emelyan.

"Hear my command," he said. "You are to build me a new cathedral on the square opposite the palace, and it must be completed by tomorrow evening. If you succeed, I shall reward you; if you fail—you will be put to death."

After hearing the tsar's order, Emelyan turned around and went home.

"Now," he thought, "my end has come."

When he got home he said to his wife: "Get ready, wife, we must flee from here, or we shall be lost!"

"Why are you so frightened?" she asked. "And why should we run away?"

"How can I help being frightened? The tsar has ordered me to build a cathedral in one day. If I do not succeed he threatens to cut off my head. There is only one thing to do —we must run away while there is still time."

But his wife would not hear of it.

"The tsar has many soldiers," she said, "they will find us wherever we go. You cannot escape him. As long as you have the strength you must obey."

"But how can I obey when it is beyond my strength?"

"Ah, my dear, don't be downcast! Eat your supper and go to bed. In the morning get up a little earlier, and all will be finished on time."

Emelyan went to bed. When his wife waked him in the morning she said:

"Go quickly, and finish the cathedral! Here are nails and a hammer. A day's work remains to be done."

When Emelyan reached the town, there in the middle of the square stood the new cathedral. It was nearly finished; Emelyan set to work to complete it, and by evening his task was fulfilled.

When the tsar woke up and looked out his palace window, to his surprise he saw a cathedral, and Emelyan walking back and forth, driving in a nail here and there. The tsar was not in the least pleased with the cathedral; he was annoyed at having no reason for executing Emelyan and taking his wife.

He summoned his servants.

"Emelyan has built the cathedral," he said, "and again I have no reason to put him to death. Even this task was not too great for him! You must devise something more ingenious. Put your wits to work, or you will be executed before he is."

This time his servants advised the tsar to command Emelyan to make a river, which should flow around the palace, with ships sailing on it. The tsar sent for Emelyan and set him the new task.

"If you can build a cathedral in one night," he said, "you will be able to do this too. Let my command be fulfilled by tomorrow. If it is not done, I shall cut off your head."

Emelyan was even more dejected than before, and he sadly went home to his wife.

"Why are you so downcast?" she asked him. "Has the tsar given you still another task?"

Emelyan told her of the tsar's order.

"We must flee," he said.

"You cannot escape his soldiers," she replied, "they will find us wherever we go. You must obey."

"But how can I obey?"

"Ah, my dear," she said to him, "there is no reason to

be sad. Eat your supper and go to bed. In the morning get up a little earlier, and all will be finished on time."

Emelyan went to bed. When his wife waked him in the morning she said:

"Go to the palace, all is ready. At the landing opposite the palace one little mound remains; take a spade and level it."

Emelyan set off. When he reached the town, there was a river encircling the palace, with ships sailing on it! He went to the landing opposite the palace, where he found an uneven place, and began to level it.

When the tsar woke up, he saw a river where none had been, and on the river ships were sailing. But neither the river nor the ships pleased the tsar; again he was annoyed at not being able to put Emelyan to death.

"There is no task he has not been able to fulfill," thought the tsar. "Now what is to be done?"

He summoned his servants and they consulted together.

"You must devise a task that is beyond Emelyan's power. No matter what you have thought of, he has been able to do it, and I can't take his wife away from him."

They thought and they thought, and at last they came to the tsar and said:

"You must send for Emelyan and say to him: 'Go who-knows-where, and bring back who-knows-what.' He'll never be able to get out of that! No matter where he goes, you can say it was the wrong place; no matter what he brings back, you can say it's the wrong thing. Then you will be able to put him to death and take his wife."

The tsar was delighted.

"This time you have thought of something clever," he said.

He sent for Emelyan and said: "Go who-knows-where, and bring back who-knows-what. And if you fail to bring it to me, I'll cut off your head."

Emelyan went home and told his wife what the tsar had said. His wife grew thoughtful.

"Well," she said, "this time they have gone so far as to teach the tsar something. Now we must act wisely."

She sat thinking for a long time. At last she said to her husband:

"You must go far away to the old peasant woman and mother of soldiers, my grandmother, and ask for her help. As soon as she gives you something, go straight to the palace, and I shall be there. I cannot escape them now; they will take me by force. But it won't be for long. If you do all the old grandmother tells you, you will soon rescue me."

And the wife prepared her husband for the journey. She gave him a little bag, and she gave him her spindle.

"Give this to her, and she will know you are my husband."

His wife then showed him the way, and Emelyan set off on his journey. After leaving the town, he came to where some soldiers were drilling, and he stopped to watch them. When the soldiers sat down to rest Emelyan went up to them and asked:

"Do you happen to know, brothers, how to go who-knows-where, and bring back who-knows-what?"

The soldiers listened to him in amazement.

"Who sent you on such a quest?" they asked.

"The tsar."

"We ourselves, from the day we became soldiers, have been going who-knows-where, and never getting there, seeking who-knows-what, and never finding it. We can't help you."

Emelyan sat with the soldiers for a while and then went on his way. He walked and he walked till he came to a forest. In the forest there was a hut, and in the hut sat an old, old woman, the mother of soldiers, weeping and spinning flax; and she did not put her fingers to her mouth to moisten them with spittle, but to her eyes to wet them with tears. When she saw Emelyan she cried out:

"What have you come for?"

Emelyan gave her the spindle and told her that his wife had sent him. The old woman immediately grew gentle and began asking him questions. Emelyan told her all about his life: about how he had married the maiden and how they had gone to live in the town; how the tsar's servants had taken him to the palace and made him work in the courtyard; how he had built the cathedral and made the river with boats sailing on it; and how he had been ordered to go who-knows-where and bring back who-knows-what.

When she had heard all this the old woman stopped weeping and began muttering to herself.

"It's clear the time has come," she said. "Very well, sit down, my son, and eat."

After Emelyan had eaten his fill, the old woman said to him:

"Take this ball, roll it before you, and follow where it goes. You will have far to go, all the way to the sea. When you reach the sea, there will be a large city. You must enter the city and ask for a night's lodging at the farthest house. There you will find what you need."

"But how shall I recognize it?"

"When you perceive what men heed more than father or mother, that is it. Seize it, and take it to the tsar. He will tell you that you have brought the wrong thing. Then you must say: 'If it is wrong, it must be destroyed.' And you will strike it a blow, carry it to the river, smash it, and throw the pieces into the water. Then you will recover your wife and dry my tears."

Emelyan said good-bye to the old grandmother and began rolling the ball before him. It rolled and rolled till it led him to the sea. By the sea there was a great city, and at the end of the city stood a tall house. There Emelyan begged a night's lodging and it was granted him.

He lay down to sleep, and early in the morning he heard the father rouse his son and tell him to go out and cut wood. But the son did not heed his father.

"It's too early," he said. "There's plenty of time."

Then, from the oven, he heard the mother say:

"Go, my son. Your father's bones ache. Would you have him go himself? It is time."

But the son only clicked his tongue and went back to sleep. No sooner had he fallen asleep than there was a rattling and a rumbling in the street. The son leaped out of bed, dressed himself, and ran out. Emelyan jumped up and ran after him to see what it was that a son heeded more than father or mother.

He saw a man walking along the street carrying a round object on his belly, and beating it with two sticks. So that was what the son had heeded! Emelyan ran up and began to examine the object. He saw that it was round, like a small tub, with a skin stretched across each end. He asked what it was called.

"A drum," they told him.

"And is it empty?"

"It is."

Emelyan marveled. He asked them to give it to him, but they refused. So he gave up asking and followed the drummer. He walked the whole day, and when the drummer lay down to sleep he seized the drum and ran off with it.

He ran and he ran till he reached home, where he thought he would find his wife; but she was gone. They had taken her to the tsar the day after Emelyan went away.

He went to the palace and told them to announce his arrival to the tsar.

"Tell him he has come who has been who-knows-where, and that he has brought back who-knows-what."

They told the tsar, but the tsar bade him return the following day. Emelyan sent a second message to the tsar.

"I have come today," he said, "and I have brought what he commanded me to bring. Let the tsar come out to me, or I shall go in to him."

The tsar appeared.

"Where have you been?" he asked.

Emelyan told him.

"That's the wrong place," said the tsar. "And what have you brought back?"

Emelyan was about to show him, but the tsar refused to look.

"That's the wrong thing," he said.

"If it's wrong it must be destroyed, and may the devil take it!"

Emelyan walked out of the palace, beating the drum as he went. No sooner had he started drumming than the tsar's entire army assembled, saluted him, and stood waiting for his orders.

From his window the tsar shouted to his soldiers not to follow Emelyan, but they did not listen, and continued to follow him. When he saw this, the tsar gave orders for Emelyan's wife to be returned to him; and he asked Emelyan to give him the drum.

"I cannot give it to you," said Emelyan. "I have been ordered to destroy it and throw it into the river."

Emelyan marched to the river with the drum, and the soldiers all followed him. There he struck it a blow, shattered it, and threw the pieces into the water. The soldiers immediately ran away. Then Emelyan took his wife and led her home.

From that day forth, the tsar ceased to trouble him, and, taking the bad with the good, he lived happily ever after.

(Tales and Stories)
1891

THE TALE OF IVAN THE FOOL AND HIS TWO BROTHERS, SEMYON THE SOLDIER AND TARAS THE BIG-BELLY, AND OF HIS SISTER MALYANA THE MUTE, AND OF THE OLD DEVIL AND THE THREE IMPS

1

In a certain kingdom of a certain realm there once lived a rich peasant. And the rich peasant had three sons: Semyon the Soldier, Taras the Big-Belly, and Ivan the Fool, and an unmarried daughter, Malyana the Mute. Semyon the Soldier went to war to serve the tsar; Taras the Big-Belly went to a merchant in town to trade; and Ivan the Fool stayed at home with his sister to break his back with hard work.

Semyon the Soldier gained high rank and an estate, and married a nobleman's daughter. His pay was large and his estate was large, but he could not make ends meet: what the husband acquired his lady wife carelessly squandered, and they never had any money.

Semyon the Soldier went to his estate to collect the income, and his steward said to him:

"Where should the money come from? We have no cattle, no tools, no horses, no cow, no plow, and no harrow; all these must be got, then there will be an income."

So Semyon the Soldier went to his father.

"Father," he said, "you are rich, but you have given me nothing. Divide what you have and give me a third part, so that I can add it to my estate."

"You brought nothing into my house," said the old man, "why should I give you a third part? It would not be fair to Ivan and the girl."

And Semyon replied: "But you know he's a fool, and she's only a deaf-and-dumb spinster. What do they need?"

Then the old man said: "Let Ivan decide."

And Ivan said: "Well, why not? Let him have it."

So Semyon the Soldier took his share of his father's goods and removed it to his own estate. And he again went off to serve the tsar.

Taras the Big-Belly also made a great deal of money, and he married into a merchant's family; but he wanted still more, so he came to his father and said:

"Give me my share."

The old man was unwilling to give Taras anything either. "You brought nothing to us," he said. "Whatever is in this house Ivan has earned. Besides, it would not be fair to him and the girl."

But Taras replied: "What good is it to him? He's a fool! He cannot marry, no one would have him; and the dumb girl doesn't need anything either. . . . Come, Ivan," he said, "give me half the grain; I won't take the tools, and I don't want any livestock, except the gray stallion—he's no good to you for plowing."

Ivan laughed and said: "Well, why not? I will work and earn more."

So they gave Taras a share too. He carted the grain off to town and took away the gray stallion. Ivan was left with one old mare to continue his peasant life as before, and to feed his father and mother.

2

Now the Old Devil was vexed that the brothers had not quarreled over the sharing but had parted amicably. He summoned three imps.

"Look here," he said, "there are three brothers: Semyon the Soldier, Taras the Big-Belly, and Ivan the Fool. They ought to have quarreled, but instead they live in peace and friendship. The Fool spoiled the whole business for me. You three go and take on those three brothers, and stir them up so they'll tear one another's eyes out. Can you do this?"

"We can," they said.

"How will you do it?"

"Like this: first we'll ruin them, and when they haven't so much as a bone to gnaw on, we'll pile them into a heap —and they'll start fighting."

"Good! I see you know your business. Now, be off, and

don't come back till they're all at loggerheads, or I'll skin you alive!"

The imps went off to a bog to consider how they should set to work. They argued and argued, each one scheming to get the easiest job. Finally they decided to draw lots to determine which brother each of them would get, and whoever finished first was to come to the aid of the others. They drew lots and set a time for another meeting in the bog to learn who had finished and whom he should help.

At the appointed time the imps met in the bog as agreed. They proceeded to explain how matters stood. The first imp told about Semyon the Soldier.

"My work is going well," he said. "Tomorrow my Semyon will go home to his father."

His comrades began questioning him. "How did you do it?" they asked.

"Well," he said, "the first thing I did was to inspire Semyon with such courage that he promised the tsar he would conquer the whole world for him. So the tsar made him commander in chief and sent him to fight the king of India. They met for battle. But during the night I dampened all the gunpowder in Semyon's army; then I went to the Indian king and made him a whole multitude of soldiers out of straw. When Semyon's soldiers saw the straw soldiers advancing on all sides, they grew timid. Semyon gave orders to fire: the guns and cannon failed to go off. His soldiers were frightened and ran like sheep, and the Indian king massacred them. Now Semyon the Soldier is disgraced, his estate has been taken from him, and tomorrow they intend to execute him. One day's work remains to be done: I have only to let him escape from prison so he can run home. Tomorrow I shall have finished. Now, tell me, which one of you needs help?"

Then the second imp described his work with Taras. "I need no help," he said, "my work is going well too. Taras can't hold out for more than a week. The first thing I did was to enlarge his belly and excite his envy. He grew so covetous that whatever he saw he wanted to buy. He spent all his money, bought vast quantities of things, and is still buying. Now he borrows in order to buy. He's so weighed down and entangled in debts that he'll never get rid of them. In a week his payments are due, but I'll turn all his goods into dung, and when he can't pay, he'll have to go home to his father."

They began to question the third imp about Ivan the Fool. "And how is your work going?" they asked.

"My work," he said, "is not going well. The first thing I did was to spit into his jug of kvas so he'd have a stomach-ache. Then I went to his field and pounded the earth till it became hard as stone, so he wouldn't be able to work it. I didn't think he'd try to plow it, but he, the fool, came out with his wooden plow and began to make a furrow. He groaned with the pain in his stomach, but he went right on plowing. I broke one plow for him, but the fool went home, got another, and continued to plow. I crawled underground and caught hold of the plowshare, but there was no holding it; he worked with a will, and the plowshare was sharp —my hands were covered with cuts! He has plowed almost the whole field, only one little strip remains to be done. Come, brothers, and help me," said the imp, "for unless we crush him all our labor will be lost. If this fool persists and succeeds with his crops, his brothers will never know want, for he'll feed them."

Semyon the Soldier's imp promised to come to his aid the next day, and on that the imps parted.

3

Ivan had plowed the entire fallow; only one little strip remained to be done, and he went out to finish it. His stomach ached, but the plowing had to be done. He released the harness ropes, turned the plow around, and started plowing. He had made one furrow and was going back when the plow began to drag as though caught on a root. It was the imp who had twined his legs around the plow-share and was holding it back.

"How strange!" thought Ivan. "There were no roots here before—but that's a root!"

He reached down and groped about in the furrow—

there was something soft! He seized it and pulled it out. It was black, like a root, but wriggled. Lo and behold!—a live imp!

"Look at that!" exclaimed Ivan. "What a horrid thing!"

He raised his arm and was about to dash the imp against the plow handle, when he heard a squeal.

"Don't hurt me!" said the imp. "I will do whatever you wish!"

"What can you do?"

"Anything you wish. You have only to tell me!"

Ivan scratched himself. "I've got a stomach-ache," he said. "Can you fix it?"

"I can," said the imp.

"Well, then cure it!"

The imp bent down and scraped about in the furrow with his claws. He pulled out a little three-pronged root and handed it to Ivan.

"Here," he said, "whoever swallows one of these roots will no longer feel pain."

Ivan tore the little root apart and swallowed one of the pieces. His stomach-ache immediately vanished.

The imp again entreated him. "Let me go!" he said. "I'll jump into the earth and never come back again!"

"Well, why not?" said Ivan. "God be with you!"

No sooner had Ivan said "God" than the imp plunged into the earth like a stone into water, and there was nothing to be seen but a hole. Ivan thrust the two remaining roots into his cap and went on with his plowing. When he reached the end of the strip he turned the plow over and went home.

He unharnessed the mare and went into the hut, and there sat his elder brother, Semyon the Soldier, and his wife at supper. Semyon had lost his estate, barely managed to escape from prison, and now had come running home to live with his father.

When Semyon saw Ivan he said: "I have come to live with you. Feed me and my wife till a new job turns up."

"Well, why not?" said Ivan. "Live here and welcome!"

Ivan was about to sit down on the bench when the lady objected to his smell.

"I cannot sup with a stinking peasant!" she said to her husband.

And Semyon the Soldier said to his brother: "My lady says you don't smell good. You had better go eat in the entry."

"Well, why not?" said Ivan. "Besides, it's time for the night watch. I must put the mare to pasture."

And he took his coat and some bread and went out to the fields with the mare.

4

Having finished his work that night, Semyon the Soldier's imp came as agreed to find Ivan's imp and help him to subdue the fool. When he reached the plowed field he searched and he searched, but his comrade was nowhere to be seen. All he could find was the hole.

"Well," he thought, "apparently my comrade has met with misfortune, and I shall have to take his place. The field is all plowed, so the fool must be tackled when he's mowing the hay."

The imp went to the meadow and flooded the entire hay-field with water, so the grass was all covered with mud.

When Ivan returned from his night watch at dawn, he sharpened his scythe, went out to the meadow, and began mowing. He had swung the scythe only once or twice when the blade became dull and had to be sharpened again. He kept struggling with it, and finally he said:

"It's no use. I'll have to go home for a tool to repair it. And I'll bring back a loaf of bread too. If it takes me a week, I won't leave till the mowing is done."

The imp heard him and thought:

"He's a hubble-bubble, this fool! You can't get around him! I'll have to try some other tricks."

Ivan returned, sharpened his scythe, and began to mow. The imp crept into the grass and kept catching the scythe by the heel, driving the tip into the ground. Hard as it was for him, Ivan kept at it till he had mowed the whole meadow except for one little patch that lay in the bog.

As he crept into the bog the imp said to himself:

"I may get my paws cut off, but I won't let him finish the mowing!"

Ivan went to the bog. To look at it the grass was not thick, yet it continually resisted the scythe. He grew angry and started swinging the scythe with all his might. The imp soon had to give in—he could not hold onto the scythe, and seeing how things were going, he decided to hide in a bush. With one sweep of the scythe Ivan grazed the bush and cut off half the imp's tail.

When he finished mowing the field Ivan told his sister to rake up the hay while he went to mow the rye.

He set off with his sickle, but the bobtailed imp had been there before him and the rye was so tangled that the sickle was of no use. Again Ivan went home; this time he returned with a pruning hook, and with this he was able to reap all the rye.

"Now," he said, "I must start on the oats."

The bobtailed imp heard him and thought: "I couldn't get the better of him on the rye, but I'll catch him on the oats! Just wait till morning!"

He hurried out to the field in the morning, but when he

got there the oats were all cut. Ivan had mowed them by night. The imp was enraged.

"That fool," he said, "has hacked me all over and worn me out. Not even in a war have I seen such disasters! He doesn't sleep, curse him! I'll get into his ricks now, and rot them all for him."

So the imp went to the stacks of rye, climbed in among the sheaves, and started rotting them. As he heated them he grew warm himself and dozed off.

Meanwhile Ivan harnessed the mare and went with his sister to cart the rye. When he got there he began pitching the rye into the cart. He had tossed up two sheaves when he thrust the fork right into the imp's back. He lifted the fork, and lo and behold!—there on the prongs, wriggling, grimacing, and struggling to get free, was a live imp with his tail cut short!

"Look at that!" exclaimed Ivan. "What a horrid thing! Back again, are you?"

"I'm another one," said the imp. "That was my brother before. I used to be with your brother Semyon."

"Well," said Ivan, "whoever you may be, you're going to get just what he got!"

He was about to dash him against the cart rail when the imp began to plead with him.

"Let me go!" he begged. "I won't do it again. And I'll do whatever you wish!"

"What can you do?"

"Why, I can make soldiers out of anything you like."

"And what are they good for?"

"For whatever you wish. They can do everything."

"Can they play tunes?"

"They can."

"Well, then," said Ivan, "make some!"

And the imp said: "Here, take a sheaf of rye, shake it over the ground, stand it up, and then say:

> " 'By decree of my fief
> No more art thou sheaf.
> Every straw that I see
> A soldier shall be.' "

Ivan took the sheaf, shook it over the ground, and repeated the imp's words. The sheaf flew apart and turned into soldiers, with a drummer and trumpeters marching at their head. Ivan burst out laughing.

"Look at that, now!" he exclaimed. "How clever! This is fine—it will amuse the girls!"

"Now will you let me go?" asked the imp.

"No," said Ivan. "I want to make them out of threshed

husks. No use wasting good grain. Teach me how to turn them into a sheaf again. Then I will thresh it."

"Just say:

> *" 'Every soldier I see*
> *Now a straw must be;*
> *As decreed by my fief,*
> *Again bound in a sheaf.' "*

As soon as Ivan had spoken these words, there was the sheaf again!

"Let me go now!" begged the imp.

"Well, why not?" said Ivan.

He hooked the imp onto the cart rail, held him down with one hand, and pulled out the fork.

"God be with you!" he said.

No sooner had he said "God" than the imp plunged into the earth like a stone into water, and there was nothing to be seen but a hole.

When Ivan got home, there sat his second brother, Taras the Big-Belly, and his wife at supper. Taras had not paid his debts, had fled from his creditors, and now had come home to live with his father.

The minute he caught sight of Ivan he said: "Look here, Ivan, feed me and my wife till I can start making money again."

"Well, why not?" said Ivan. "Live here and welcome!"

Then Ivan took off his coat and sat down at the table.
But the merchant's wife spoke up:

"I cannot eat with the fool," she said. "He reeks of sweat!"

Taras the Big-Belly said to Ivan: "You don't smell good, Ivan. You'd better go eat in the entry."

"Well, why not?" said Ivan.

And he took some bread and went out to the yard.

"Besides, it's time for the night watch," he said. "I must put the mare to pasture."

5

Taras's imp finished his work that night and came as agreed to help his comrades with Ivan the Fool. When he arrived at the plowed field, he searched and he searched, but no one was there. All he could find was a hole. He went to the meadow; there in the bog was a tail, and in the midst of the rotting rye he found a second hole.

"Well," he thought, "it's clear that my comrades have met with misfortune. I shall have to replace them and tackle the fool myself."

The imp went to look for Ivan. But Ivan had already gathered the crops and was cutting wood in the grove.

The two brothers had begun to feel cramped living together, so they told the fool he could keep the hut for himself, and ordered him to go out and cut wood and build new houses for them.

The imp ran to the wood, crawled in among the branches, and began to hinder Ivan from felling trees. Ivan undercut one tree so that it should fall clear, but it fell the wrong way and got caught in some branches. He cut a pole with which to turn the tree over, and with great difficulty brought it down. He then set to work to fell another tree— again the same thing.

Ivan had expected to cut down half a hundred young

trees, but he had not cut a dozen when night fell over the farm. He was exhausted. Steam rose from him and spread like a mist through the woods, but he would not give up. He undercut still another tree, but his back ached so he could stand it no longer; he drove his ax into the tree and sat down to rest.

When the imp heard that Ivan had stopped working, he was overjoyed.

"At last," he thought, "he's worn out! Now he'll give up, and I can rest too."

He merrily seated himself astride a bough. But Ivan got up, pulled out his ax, and struck the tree with such force from the opposite side that it instantly came down with a crash. The imp, caught off guard, failed to get free in time, and his leg was wedged under a branch. Ivan began stripping the tree, and lo and behold!—a live imp! Ivan was amazed.

"Look at that!" he exclaimed. "What a horrid thing! Are you back again?"

"I'm another one," said the imp. "I used to be with your brother Taras."

"Well, whoever you may be, you're going to get just what he got!"

Ivan swung his ax and was about to strike him dead with the handle. The imp began to plead with him.

"Don't hit me," he begged. "I'll do whatever you wish!"

"What can you do?"

"I can make money for you—as much as you like!"

"Well, then," said Ivan, "make some!"

And the imp showed him how to do it. "Take a leaf from this oak, rub it, and gold will fall from your hands."

Ivan took some leaves and rubbed them together, and a shower of gold fell from his hands.

"That's good!" he said. "The boys will have a fine time with that!"

"Let me go now," said the imp.

Ivan took his pole and freed the imp.

"God be with you!" he said.

No sooner had he said "God" than the imp plunged into the earth like a stone into water, and there was nothing to be seen but a hole.

6

The brothers had built their houses and were living apart. After harvesting the crops, Ivan brewed beer and invited his brothers to celebrate with him. But they refused to be his guests.

"What have we to do with peasant revels?" they said.

So Ivan entertained the peasants and their wives. He himself drank heartily; and when he was tipsy he went into the street where they were dancing and singing and told the women to sing a song in his honor.

"And I will give you something you have never in your lives seen before."

The women laughed and sang a song in praise of him. When they had finished they said: "Now give it to us!"

"I'll bring it at once," Ivan said. And he took up a sack and ran to the woods.

"What a fool he is!" laughed the women. And they soon forgot all about him.

But suddenly Ivan came running back with the sack full of something.

"Shall I share it?" he asked them.

"Yes, share it!"

Ivan took a handful of gold and flung it to the women. How they threw themselves on it! And how the men sprang forward, snatching and tearing at one another to get the gold! One old woman was nearly trampled to death. Ivan laughed at them.

"Ah, you fools!" he said. "Why crush the old granny? Don't be so rough—I'll give you more."

He began tossing more gold pieces to them, and they all crowded around him. When the sack was empty they still begged for more.

"That's all," said Ivan. "Some other time I'll give you more. Now for a dance! Let's have a tune!"

The women struck up a song.

"Your tunes are no good!" said Ivan.

"Where will you find better?" they asked.

"I'll show you, right now!"

Ivan went to the barn, pulled out a sheaf and threshed it, then shook it over the ground, stood it up, tapped it, and said:

> *"By decree of my fief*
> *No more art thou sheaf.*
> *Every straw that I see*
> *A soldier shall be."*

The sheaf flew apart and turned into soldiers playing drums and trumpets.

Ivan ordered the soldiers to play tunes, and led them out into the street. The people were amazed. When the soldiers had finished playing, Ivan led them back into the barn—after forbidding the peasants to follow him—and turned them back into a sheaf. Then he flung the sheaf onto the pile, and went home and lay down in the stable to sleep.

7

The next morning, hearing of these things, the elder brother, Semyon the Soldier, came to Ivan.

"Tell me," he said, "where did you get those soldiers? And where have you taken them?"

"Why do you want to know?" asked Ivan.

"What do you mean, why? With soldiers you can do anything—you can win a kingdom for yourself!"

Ivan was astonished. "Really?" he asked. "Why didn't you tell me this long ago? I'll make you as many as you like. Luckily the girl and I threshed a lot!"

Ivan took his brother to the threshing floor and said: "Look here, I'll make soldiers for you, but then you must take them away; if we had to feed them, they'd gobble up the whole village in one day."

Semyon the Soldier promised to lead the soldiers away, and Ivan began making them. He tapped one sheaf on the floor—a company appeared! He tapped another—another company! He made so many that the whole field was covered with them.

"Well, that will do, won't it?"

"It will. Thank you, Ivan."

"All right," said Ivan. "If you need any more, come back and I'll make them. There's plenty of straw still."

Semyon the Soldier mustered his troops, took command of his army, and marched off to make war.

No sooner had Semyon the Soldier gone than Taras the Big-Belly came along. He too had heard of what happened the day before.

"Tell me," he said to his brother, "where did you get all that gold? If I had so much free money I could make it bring in more money from all over the world."

Ivan was astonished. "Really?" he said, "Why didn't you tell me this long ago? I will make you as much as you like."

His brother was delighted. "Give me at least three sack-fuls," he said.

"Well, why not? Come with me to the forest. But first let us harness the mare—you won't be able to carry it all."

They went to the forest and Ivan began rubbing oak leaves. He made a great heap of gold.

"That will do, won't it?"

Taras was overjoyed. "It will do for now," he said. "Thank you, Ivan."

"All right," replied Ivan. "If you need any more, come back and I'll make it for you. There are plenty of leaves left."

Taras the Big-Belly gathered up a whole cartload of money and went off to trade.

So the two brothers went away: Semyon to fight, and Taras to trade. Semyon the Soldier conquered a kingdom for himself, and Taras the Big-Belly made a lot of money buying and selling.

When the brothers met, Semyon told Taras how he had got his soldiers, and Taras told Semyon how he had got his money.

And Semyon the Soldier said to his brother: "I have conquered a kingdom, and I could live well, but I have no money to feed my soldiers."

Then Taras the Big-Belly said: "And I have amassed a great heap of money, but my trouble is that I have no one to guard it."

"Let us go to our brother Ivan," said Semyon the Soldier. "I'll order him to make more soldiers, then I'll give them to you to guard your money; and you order him to make more money, and give it to me to feed my soldiers."

They went to Ivan, and when they got there Semyon said:

"I haven't enough soldiers, brother. Make me some more—change a couple of haystacks or so."

Ivan shook his head.

"No more," he said. "I am not going to make you any more soldiers."

"Why not? You promised!"

"I did. But I won't make any more."

"Why won't you, you fool?"

"Because your soldiers killed a man. A few days ago, when I was plowing near the road, a woman came by with a coffin on her cart. She was wailing, and I asked her: 'Who died?' She said: 'Semyon the Soldier killed my husband in the war.' I thought soldiers were for making music, but they have killed a man. I will give you no more."

And the fool stood firm and would make no more soldiers.

Then Taras the Big-Belly began to plead with him to make more gold. Ivan shook his head.

"No more," he said. "I am not going to make you any more gold."

"Why not? You promised!"

"I did. But I won't make any more."

"Why won't you, you fool?"

"Because your gold pieces took away Mikhailovna's cow."

"Took it away? How?"

"Just took it away. Mikhailovna had a cow, and her children used to drink the milk. The other day they came to me asking for milk. 'Where is your cow?' I said. 'The

steward of Taras the Big-Belly came to Mama and gave
her three pieces of gold, and she gave him our cow. Now
we have no milk to drink.' I thought you only wanted to
play with the gold, but you have taken the children's cow
away from them. I will give you no more."

And the fool stood firm and would make no more gold.

So the brothers went away and considered how to
remedy their difficulties.

"I'll tell you what we'll do," said Semyon the Soldier.
"You give me money to feed my soldiers, and I'll give you
half my kingdom and soldiers to guard your money."

Taras agreed. So the brothers divided their possessions,
and both became tsars, and both were rich.

8

Meanwhile Ivan was living at home, feeding his father
and mother, and working in the fields with the deaf-and-
dumb girl.

Now it happened one day that Ivan's old watchdog fell
ill; she grew mangy and appeared to be dying. Ivan felt
sorry for her and got bread from his sister to take out to
her.

When he threw the bread to the dog, his cap, which was
torn, fell off, and a little root fell out of it. The dog gobbled
up the root along with the bread, and no sooner had she
swallowed it than she jumped up and started to play, bark-
ing and wagging her tail. She was cured!

The father and mother saw this and were amazed. "How
did you cure the dog?" they asked Ivan.

"I had two little roots that cure any pain," he said, "and
she swallowed one of them."

About that time it happened that the tsar's daughter fell
ill, and the tsar proclaimed in every town and village that
whoever might cure her would receive a reward, and if

he were a bachelor, he would receive her hand in marriage. The proclamation was heard in Ivan's village too.

Ivan's father and mother called him in and said: "Have you heard what the tsar has proclaimed? You said you had one more little root; go and heal the tsar's daughter, and you shall be happy the rest of your life."

"Well, why not?" said Ivan.

And he got ready to go. They dressed him in his best, and he had just gone out the door when he caught sight of a beggar woman with a crippled arm.

"I have heard that you heal people," she said. "Heal my arm. I cannot even put on my own boots."

"Well, why not?" said Ivan.

He took out the little root, gave it to the beggar woman, and told her to swallow it. She did as she was told and was instantly cured, and she began to move her arm about freely.

When Ivan's father and mother came out to accompany him on his journey to the tsar, they heard that he had given away his last root and now had nothing with which to cure the tsar's daughter. They began to upbraid him.

"You take pity on a beggar woman," they said, "but for the tsar's daughter you have no pity!"

But Ivan felt pity for the tsar's daughter as well, and he harnessed the mare, threw some straw into the cart, and set off.

"Where are you going, fool?"

"I am going to heal the tsar's daughter."

"When you have nothing to heal her with?"

"Well, why not?" said Ivan, and drove off.

When he reached the tsar's palace, no sooner had he set foot on the threshold than the tsar's daughter was cured.

The tsar was overjoyed. He had Ivan brought before him, dressed him in fine robes, and rewarded him.

"Be my son-in-law," he said to him.

"Well, why not?" said Ivan. And he married the tsar's daughter.

Not long afterwards the tsar died, and Ivan became tsar. Now all three brothers were tsars.

9

The three brothers lived and reigned.

The eldest brother, Semyon the Soldier, prospered. He conscripted real soldiers to add to his straw soldiers. Throughout his entire realm he decreed that for every ten houses one man must go into the army, and every soldier had to be of great height, clean-bodied and clear-eyed. He gathered many such men and trained them, and when anyone opposed him, he immediately sent out his soldiers, and he did whatever he wished. Soon the people began to fear him.

His life was a pleasant one: anything he fancied, anything that caught his eye, was his. He simply sent out his soldiers, and they seized and brought back to him all he desired.

Taras the Big-Belly prospered too. He lost none of the money he got from Ivan, but greatly increased it. And he too established order in his kingdom. He kept his own money in coffers, and collected more and more from his people. He taxed every soul in his realm; he taxed them for vodka and beer, for bast shoes, for leg wrappings, for dress trimmings. And whatever he fancied was his. People would bring anything to him, perform any work for him—everyone wanted his money.

Ivan the Fool did not fare badly either. As soon as he had buried his father-in-law, he took off his royal robes, gave them to his wife to put away in a chest, and put on his hempen shirt, breeches, and bast shoes. And he began working again.

"It's dull," he said, "and I'm growing a belly; I have no appetite, and can't sleep."

He sent for his father and mother and his sister the mute to come and live with him; then he set to work.

"But you are the tsar!" they all said to him.

"Well, why not?" he replied. "Even a tsar must eat."

One of his ministers came to him and said: "There is no money to pay salaries."

"Then don't pay them."

"But the people will stop serving."

"Let them stop serving," said Ivan. "If they stop serving they will be free to work. Let them cart away the manure; they've piled up enough of it."

People came before him to be tried.

"He stole my money," said one.

"Well, why not?" said Ivan. "That shows he needs it."

Everyone recognized that Ivan was a fool.

"They say you're a fool," his wife said to him.

"Well, why not?" said Ivan.

His wife thought and thought about this, but she too was a fool.

"Why should I go against my husband?" she said. "Where the needle goes the thread must follow."

She took off her royal robes, put them away in a chest, and went to the mute girl to learn how to work. She soon learned and began helping her husband.

All the wise men left Ivan's kingdom; only the fools remained. They lived and worked, feeding themselves and all good people.

10

Now the Old Devil waited and waited to learn how the imps had ruined the three brothers; but no news came from them, so he went to find out for himself. He searched and he searched, but they were nowhere to be seen; all he could find were the three holes.

"Well," he thought, "clearly, they have not succeeded. I shall have to tackle it myself."

He went to look for the three brothers, but they were no longer in their old places; he found them in their various kingdoms, all three alive and reigning. This seemed outrageous to the Old Devil.

"I'll take care of this matter myself!"

First of all he went to Tsar Semyon. He did not appear in his own form, but turned himself into a general before going to the palace.

"I hear, Tsar Semyon, that you are a great warrior," he said. "I am thoroughly trained in that work, and I should like to serve you."

Tsar Semyon asked him some questions, and finding him to be a clever man, took him into his service.

The new general began teaching Tsar Semyon how to build a strong army.

"In the first place, we must enlist more men," he said, "otherwise you will have too many mischievous idlers in your realm. You must call up all the young men without exception, then your army will be five times its present size. In the second place, we must have new guns and cannon. I will provide you with guns that will fire a hun-

dred bullets at once—like a spatter of peas! And I will
provide cannon that will consume everything with flame—
men, horses, walls—they will burn up anything!"

After listening to the new general, Tsar Semyon gave
orders that every youth without exception be taken into
the army; he had factories built to make the new guns and
cannon; and then went to war with a neighboring ruler. As
soon as the other army came forth to meet him, Tsar Semyon gave orders to his soldiers to fire bullets and hurl flame
from their cannon. At one blow he crippled or consumed
half the army. The neighboring ruler took fright and sur-
rendered his realm. Semyon the Tsar was overjoyed.

"Now," he said, "I will conquer the king of India."

But the king of India had heard about Tsar Semyon, and
had adopted all of his inventions, adding a few of his own.
He began by taking not only the young men as soldiers,
but all the unmarried women as well, and his army was
even larger than Semyon's. Besides copying Semyon's guns
and cannon, he had invented a method of flying through
the air and dropping explosive bombs from above.

Tsar Semyon set out to wage war on the Indian king,
expecting to fight as he had before—but the once sharp
scythe had lost its edge. The king of India did not let
Semyon's army come within firing distance before he had
sent his women soldiers through the air to launch explosive
bombs. The women sprayed bombs on the army like borax
on cockroaches. The entire army took flight, and Semyon
the Tsar was left all alone. The Indian king took Semyon's
kingdom, and he had to escape as best he could.

Having finished with one of the brothers, the Old Devil
went on to Tsar Taras. He changed himself into a merchant

and settled in Taras's realm. He established a business and spent money freely, paying the highest prices for everything. The people all rushed to get his money, and he put so much of it into circulation that they settled the arrears on their taxes, and even began paying them on time.

Tsar Taras was delighted. "Thanks to this merchant, I now have more money than ever, and life grows better all the time."

And Tsar Taras began to devise new projects. He conceived the idea of having a new palace built for himself, and announced that the people were to bring him wood and stone and start working. He set high prices for everything, and thought they would come in crowds as before to get his money. But no! They took their wood and their stone to the new merchant, and the workmen all flocked to him. If Tsar Taras raised his prices, the merchant raised his still higher. The tsar had a great deal of money, but the merchant had more, and he overbid him at every point. Work on the royal palace soon came to a halt.

A park had been laid out by the tsar, and when autumn came he sent for people to come and plant it, but no one came: they were all engaged in digging a pond for the merchant.

Winter came and Tsar Taras wanted to buy sables for a new overcoat. The emissary he sent to buy them returned.

"There are no sables," he said. "The merchant offered a higher price. He has bought up all the furs and made carpets of them."

When Tsar Taras wanted to buy stallions, his emissary came back and told him that the merchant had all the good stallions; they were carrying water to fill his pond.

And so all the tsar's projects came to a standstill. No one would work for him; everyone was working for the merchant. They brought him nothing but the merchant's money to pay their taxes.

Tsar Taras had amassed so much money he had no place to put it, and his life became miserable. He gave up making plans and wanted nothing more than to live somehow—but even that was impossible. There was a shortage of everything. His cooks, coachmen, and valets all left him to go to the merchant's; and before long he lacked even food. When he sent to the market there was nothing to be had—the merchant had bought up everything. Nothing was ever brought to him except money for taxes.

Tsar Taras became so infuriated that he banished the merchant from his realm. But the merchant settled just across the border and continued as before, and his money still drew everything away from the tsar.

Things were going badly for Tsar Taras; he had not eaten for days, and it was rumored that the merchant was

now boasting that he would even buy the tsar's wife! Tsar Taras lost heart and did not know what to do.

Then Semyon the Soldier came to him and said: "Help me! I have been defeated by the king of India."

But Tsar Taras was at the end of his rope. "I myself have not eaten for two days," he said.

11

Having finished with two of the brothers, the Old Devil now turned to Ivan. He changed himself into a general, appeared before Ivan, and began by urging him to raise an army.

"It is not fitting that a tsar should be without an army," he said. "You have only to command me and I will gather soldiers from among your people and form an army."

Ivan heard him out and then said: "Well, why not? Go ahead! But train them to play tunes skillfully—that's what I like."

The Old Devil went throughout the kingdom trying to enlist volunteers. He told them that when they came for the head-shaving each man would receive a measure of vodka and a red cap.

The fools only laughed at him. "We have plenty of liquor," they said, "we make it ourselves. And as for caps, the women make us all kinds—even striped ones with tassels."

And no one would enlist. The Old Devil went back to Ivan.

"Your fools won't come as volunteers," he said. "They'll have to be brought in by force."

"Well, why not?" said Ivan. "Bring them in by force."

The Old Devil made it known that all fools were required to enlist as soldiers, and whoever refused would be put to death by Ivan.

The fools came to the general and said: "You say that we will be put to death if we don't enlist; but you don't tell us what will happen if we do enlist. We have heard that soldiers also get killed."

"Yes, that happens."

Hearing this the fools became obstinate. "We won't go!" they said. "Better to stay home and be put to death, since it can't be avoided anyway."

"Fools!" said the Old Devil. "You fools! A soldier may or may not be killed; but if you don't enlist, Tsar Ivan is certain to put you to death."

The fools pondered; then they went to Tsar Ivan the Fool.

"A general appeared," they said, "and ordered us all to become soldiers. 'If you enlist,' he says, 'you may be killed, or you may not be killed; and if you don't enlist, Tsar Ivan is certain to put you to death.' Is this true?"

Ivan laughed. "How could I, alone, put all of you to death? If I weren't a fool I could explain this to you, but as it is, I don't understand it myself."

"Then we won't go," they said.

"Well, why not?" said Ivan. "Don't go."

The fools went to the general and refused to become soldiers.

The Old Devil saw that his plan would not work, so he went to the king of Tarakan and tried to gain his good will.

"Let us go to war," he said, "and conquer Tsar Ivan. He has no money, it's true, but he has plenty of grain and cattle, and all sorts of other goods."

The king of Tarakan agreed to go to war. He assembled a large army, put his guns and cannon in shape, and marched to the border of Ivan's kingdom.

The people came to Ivan and said: "The king of Tarakan is coming to make war on us."

"Well, why not?" said Ivan. "Let him come."

The king of Tarakan crossed the border and sent out his scouts to find Ivan's army. They searched and they searched, but they could find no army. Then they waited and waited—surely an army would turn up somewhere. But there was not even a rumor of one—no one to fight!

The king of Tarakan sent men to take the villages. When they came to a village all the fools, both men and women, bounded out to gaze at the soldiers and marvel. The soldiers took away their grain and their cattle, and the fools let it go without even resisting. The soldiers went on to the next village, and the same thing happened; and the next day and the next—every place was the same: the people handed over everything to them. Not only did they fail to defend themselves, but they even invited the soldiers to stay with them.

"If life is so miserable in your country, dear friends, come and live here with us," they said.

The soldiers marched on and on—and still no army, only people living and feeding themselves and others, never resisting, but always welcoming the soldiers and inviting them to stay.

It became dull work for them, and they went to their king and said: "We can't fight here. Lead us elsewhere. A war would be fine, but we can't make war here. This is like cutting jelly!"

The king of Tarakan grew angry and commanded his soldiers to overrun the whole kingdom, to lay waste the villages, burn the houses and grain, and slaughter the cattle.

"If my orders are not carried out," he said, "you will all be executed!"

The soldiers were frightened; they began at once to do as their king ordered. They burned the houses and grain, and slaughtered the cattle. And still the fools offered no resistance, but only stood by and wept: the old men wept, the old women wept, and the little children wept too.

"Why do you injure us?" they asked. "Why are you destroying good things? If you want them, why don't you take them for yourselves?"

At last the soldiers could bear it no longer; they refused to go on, and the entire army disbanded.

12

The Old Devil also went away, having failed to overcome Ivan with his soldiers.

Then he transformed himself into a fine gentleman and came back and settled in Ivan's kingdom. He now planned to catch Ivan the way he had caught Taras the Big-Belly—with money.

"I want to do you a good turn," he said to Ivan, "to teach you wit and wisdom. I shall build a house here, and establish a business."

"Well, why not?" said Ivan. "Live here and welcome!"

The next morning the fine gentleman appeared in the public square with a big bag of gold and a sheet of paper.

"You people live like swine," he said. "I am going to teach you how to live properly. Build me a house according to this plan. Work as I direct you, and I shall pay you with these gold coins."

He showed them the gold. The fools were astounded. They did not use money, but bartered their goods or paid one another in labor. They gazed at the gold pieces in wonder.

"Those are pretty little things!" they said.

They began to exchange their goods and their labor for gold pieces. The Old Devil spent money as freely as he had done in Taras's kingdom, and the people brought all sorts of things, and did all sorts of work for it. The Old Devil was delighted.

"My work is progressing," he thought. "Now I shall ruin the fool as I ruined Taras. I shall buy him up, strip him of everything!"

But the fools no sooner collected their gold pieces than they gave them away: the women all wore them as necklaces, the girls plaited them into their hair, and the children played with them in the streets. Once everyone had enough of them, the men would not take any more. But the fine gentleman's mansion was not yet half built, and his grain and cattle were not yet stocked for the year, so he sent word to the people to come back and work, to cart grain and bring cattle, and that he had plenty of gold to pay for everything.

No one came to work for him, and no one brought him anything. A little girl or boy would run up to exchange an egg for a gold piece, but no one else ever came, and soon he had nothing to eat.

Being hungry, the fine gentleman went through the village trying to buy something for dinner. He thrust his head in at one door and offered a gold piece for a fowl, but the housewife refused it.

"I have lots of them," she said.

He tried to give a gold piece to a poor woman in exchange for a herring.

"It's no good to me, kind sir," she said. "I have no children to play with it. And I already have three of them that I took as curiosities."

He went to a peasant's hut for bread, but the peasant would not take any money.

"I don't need it," he said. "If you are begging in Christ's name, then wait here, and I'll tell the old woman to cut you a piece of bread."

The Old Devil spat and ran away from the peasant. Let alone the idea of begging in Christ's name, just hearing Him mentioned was worse than the cut of a knife.

And so he got no bread either. Everyone had gold, and no matter where he went no one would give him anything for money.

"Bring us something else, or come and work," they would say, "or else take what you need in Christ's name."

But the Devil had nothing but money; he was unwilling to work, and he could not possibly take anything in Christ's name. He grew furious.

"I will give you money—what more do you want?" he asked them. "You can buy anything, hire anyone, with gold!"

The fools would not listen to him. "No," they said, "we don't need it. We have no bills and no taxes—what should we do with it?"

The Old Devil was forced to go to bed without supper.

Ivan the Fool heard of this matter. People came to him and asked:

"What shall we do? A fine gentleman has appeared who likes to eat and drink well and dress nicely, but does not want to work nor to beg in Christ's name; he only wants to give gold pieces to everyone. At first we gave him everything he wanted, but we have enough gold pieces, and now we don't give him anything. What are we to do with him? He may die of hunger."

Ivan listened to them and then said:

"Well, he must be fed. Let him go from farmhouse to farmhouse as the shepherds do."

There was nothing to be done, the Old Devil had to start going from one farmhouse to another. In due time he turned up at Ivan's house. When he came in, the mute girl was preparing dinner. She had often been deceived by the lazy, who came early to dinner, their work unfinished, and ate up all the gruel. She had learned to recognize the idlers by their hands: those who had calluses she seated at the table, the others were given the scraps. The Old Devil slipped into a place at the table, but the mute girl seized his hands and examined them. There were no calluses; he had clean, smooth hands with long claws. She grunted and dragged him away from the table.

Then Ivan's wife spoke to him: "You must excuse her, fine gentleman," she said. "My sister-in-law does not allow anyone without calluses to sit at the table. Just wait till the others have eaten, then you can have what is left."

The Old Devil was offended that in a tsar's house he should be fed like the swine.

"That's a stupid law you have here," he said to Ivan, "that everyone must work with his hands. And you devised it out of stupidity. Do you think people work only with their hands? What do you think clever people work with?"

"How are we fools to know?" replied Ivan. "We're used to doing most of our work with our hands and our backs."

"That's because you are fools," said the Old Devil. "But I will teach you how to work with your heads; then you will realize that it's more profitable to work with the head than with the hands."

Ivan was amazed. "Well," he said, "no wonder we're called fools!"

"But it's not easy," the Old Devil began, "to work with

your head. Here you give me nothing to eat because I have
no calluses on my hands; but what you don't know is that
it's a hundred times harder to work with your head. Sometimes the head even splits."

Ivan pondered. "Then why torture yourself, my dear
friend?" he asked. "That can't be easy—to have your head
split! Wouldn't it be better to do easier work, with your
hands and your back?"

And the Devil replied: "I torture myself out of pity for
you fools. If I didn't torture myself you would remain
fools forever. But having worked with my head, I will now
teach you."

Ivan marveled. "Do teach us," he said, "so that the next
time our hands are worn out we can shift to our heads."

The Devil promised to teach them.

And Ivan announced throughout his realm that a fine
gentleman had appeared who would teach everyone how
to work with his head; that it was more profitable to work
with the head than with the hands; and that all must come
and learn.

Now there was in Ivan's kingdom a high belfry with a
steep staircase leading up to a watchtower at the top. Ivan
took the gentleman up there so that he would be visible to
all the people.

The gentleman stood up in the tower and began to
speak. The fools gathered to watch. They thought he was
going to show them how they could do their work with
their heads instead of their hands, but in fact the Old Devil
used nothing but words to explain how to live without
doing any work.

The fools could make nothing of this. They continued
to watch him for a while and then went on about their
business.

The Old Devil stood in the tower the whole day, and
all through the following day, continually talking. He grew
hungry, but it never occurred to the fools to bring him
bread. They thought that if he could work better with his
head than his hands it would be a mere trifle for his head
to provide him with a little bread.

The Old Devil stood in the tower still another day, always talking. The people would approach him, stand and
stare, then walk away.

"Well, has the gentleman started working with his head?" inquired Ivan.

"Not yet," they replied. "He's still jabbering."

The Old Devil stood in the tower one more day, and then, having grown weak, he staggered and struck his head against a pillar. One of the fools saw him and told Ivan's wife, and she ran to her husband who was plowing.

"Come and see," she said. "They say the gentleman has begun working with his head!"

Ivan was surprised. "Really?" he said.

He turned the horse around and went to the belfry. By the time he got there the Old Devil was so weak from hunger he was staggering about and knocking his head against the pillars. Just as Ivan drew near, he stumbled and fell, and came crashing headfirst down the staircase, counting each step with his head.

"Well," said Ivan, "the fine gentleman was telling the

truth when he said the head sometimes splits. It's not just calluses you get—this work leaves lumps!"

The Old Devil had shot down the staircase and landed with his head stuck fast in the earth. Ivan went closer to see how much work he had done, when suddenly the earth opened, and the Old Devil fell through; and there was nothing to be seen but a hole.

Ivan scratched himself.

"Look at that!" he said. "What a horrid thing! It's him again! But he must be the father of them all! That's a big one!"

Ivan still lives to this day, and people flock to his kingdom to live. His brothers have come back again, and he feeds them too.

And whenever anyone comes and says: "Feed us," Ivan says: "Well, why not? Stay with us and welcome. We have plenty of everything."

There is just one custom that is always observed in his kingdom: he who has calluses sits at the table; he who has none eats the scraps.

(Tales and Stories)
1906

SELECTED BIBLIOGRAPHY

OTHER WORKS BY LEO TOLSTOY

Childhood, 1852   Novel
The Raid, 1853   Story (Signet CD56)
Boyhood, 1854   Novel
Sevastopol, 1855   Stories
Two Hussars, 1856   Novel
Youth, 1857   Novel
Family Happiness, 1859   Story (Signet CD13)
The Cossacks, 1863   Novel (Signet CD56)
War and Peace, 1869   Novel
Anna Karenina, 1877   Novel (Signet CT34)
The Memoirs of a Madman, 1884   Story
A Confession, 1884   Essay
The Death of Ivan Ilych, 1886   Story (Signet CD13)
The Power of Darkness, 1889   Play
The Kreutzer Sonata, 1889   Story (Signet CD13)
Master and Man, 1895   Story (Signet CD13)
What Is Art?   1896   Essay
Father Sergius, 1896   Story
Resurrection, 1899   Novel (Signet CT63)
The Devil, 1911   Story

SELECTED CRITICISM AND BIOGRAPHY

Arnold, Matthew. *Essays in Criticism: Second Series.* New York: St Martin's Press, Inc., 1938.
Asquith, Cynthia. *Married to Tolstoy.* Boston: Houghton Mifflin Company, 1961.
Berlin, Isaiah. *The Hedgehog and the Fox: An Essay on Tolstoy's View of History.* London: George Weidenfeld & Nicholson; New York: Simon and Schuster, 1953. The New American Library (Mentor Books), 1957.
Farrell, James T. *Literature and Morality.* New York: The Vanguard Press, Inc., 1947.
Gibian, George. *Tolstoy and Shakespeare.* New York: Humanities Press (paper), 1957.

Gorky, Maxim. *Reminiscences of Tolstoy, Chekhov, and Andreyev.* New York: The Viking Press, Inc. (Compass Books), 1959.

Hoffman, Modest and Andre Pierre. *By Deeds of Truth: The Life of Leo Tolstoy.* New York: Orion Press, Inc., 1958.

Mann, Thomas. *Three Essays.* New York: Alfred A. Knopf, Inc., 1929; London: Martin Secker Ltd., 1932.

Maude, Aylmer. *The Life of Tolstoy.* New York and London: Oxford University Press, 1931.

Mirsky, Dmitri S. *History of Russian Literature,* ed. by Francis J. Whitfield. New York: Alfred A. Knopf, 1949 (Vintage Books).

Simmons, Ernest J. *Leo Tolstoy.* Boston: Little, Brown and Company, 1945. New York: Alfred A. Knopf, Inc. (Vintage Books), 1960.

Steiner, George. *Tolstoy or Dostoevsky: An Essay in the Old Criticism.* New York: Alfred A. Knopf, Inc., 1959.

Stilman, Leon, ed. *Leo Tolstoy: Last Diaries.* New York: G. P. Putnam's Sons (Capricorn Books), 1960.

Zweig, Stefan. *Adepts in Self-Portraiture: Casanova, Stendhal, Tolstoy.* New York: Viking Press, Inc., 1928.

NOTE ON THE TEXT

Most of the fables and fairy tales here collected were originally written by Tolstoy for the "Primers" he prepared to teach Russian peasants' children to read. Some of the tales, such as "How the Imp Made Amends for the Crust of Bread," based on an ancient White Russian folktale, were inspired by themes and stories that Tolstoy found in a volume of folk stories collected by A. N. Afanasev. "Emelyan and the Empty Drum," also inspired by Afanasev's book, was first published in 1892 in a collection called *Help for the Hungry,* issued for the purpose of raising funds to aid victims of the great famine which swept the Russian countryside that year. In 1903, Tolstoy was asked by Sholom Aleichem to contribute three stories for another publication; in this case the proceeds were to help the victims of an anti-Jewish pogrom in Kishinev. Tolstoy had written an open letter to the tsar accusing his government of being directly responsible for the pogrom. "The Three Questions" and "Esarhaddon, King of Assyria" are two of the three stories he sent to Aleichem. They were first published in Yiddish in 1903, then later in Russian that same year.

SIGNET CLASSICS by Russian Authors

SIGNET CLASSICS by Other European Authors

ATALA AND RENÉ *by François René de Chateaubriand*
Newly translated, with a Foreword by Walter J. Cobb.
(#CD103—50¢)

PLATERO AND I *by Juan Ramon Jiminez*
Translated by William and Mary Roberts. Introduction by
William Roberts.   (#CD17—50¢)

NIGHT FLIGHT *by Antoine de St. Exupèry*
Translated by Stuart Gilbert. Foreword by Andre Gide.
(#CD46—50¢)

THE TRAVELS OF MARCO POLO
Edited, with an Introduction by Milton Rugoff. (#CD97—50¢)

MANON LESCAUT *by Abbé Prevost*
Newly translated, with an Introduction by Donald Frame.
(#CP96—60¢)

DARKNESS AT NOON *by Arthur Koestler*
Translated by Daphne Hardy. Foreword by Peter Viereck.
(#CD64—50¢)

DEATH OF A NOBODY *by Jules Romains*
Foreword by Maurice Natanson.   (#CD54—50¢)

THE STORY OF GOSTA BERLING *by Selma Lagerlöf*
Newly translated, with an Afterword by Robert Bly.
(#CT125—75¢)

SIGNET CLASSICS by English and American Authors